Bright

Bright

Duanwad Pimwana

Translated from Thai by Mui Poopoksakul

TWO LINES
PRESS

Originally published as: *Changsamran*
© 2002 by Pimjai Juklin
Translation © 2019 by Mui Poopoksakul

Two Lines Press
582 Market Street, Suite 700, San Francisco, CA 94104
www.twolinespress.com

ISBN 978-1-931883-80-1

Cover design by Gabriele Wilson
Cover photo © Jessica Sevey
Typeset by Jessica Sevey
Printed in the United States of America

Poem ("Toy on Target") from *100 Poems without
a Country* by Erich Fried. New York: Red Dust, Inc., 2007.

Library of Congress Cataloging-in-Publication Data
Names: Duanwad Pimwana, author. | Poopoksakul, Mui, translator. |
Translation of: Duanwad Pimwana. Changsamran.
Title: Bright / Duanwad Pimwana ; translated by Mui Poopoksakul.
Other titles: Changsamran. English
Description: San Francisco, CA : Two Lines Press, 2019.
Identifiers: LCCN 2018039546 | ISBN 9781931883801 (pbk.)
Classification: LCC PL4209.D84 C4713 2019 | DDC 895.9/134--dc23
LC record available at https://lccn.loc.gov/2018039546

1 3 5 7 9 10 8 6 4 2

This book was published with support
from the National Endowment for the Arts.

ART WORKS.
arts.gov

Mrs. Tongjan's Community

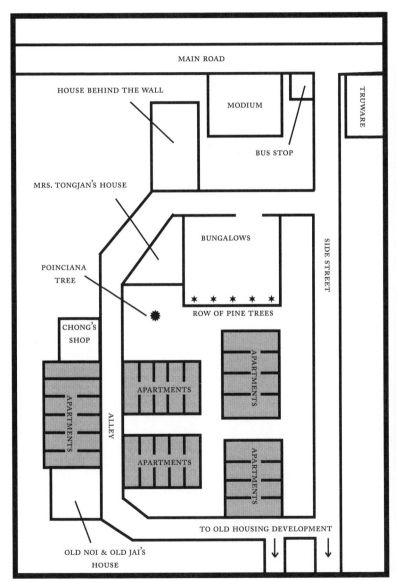

MAIN ROAD

HOUSE BEHIND THE WALL

MODIUM

TRUWARE

BUS STOP

MRS. TONGJAN'S HOUSE

BUNGALOWS

SIDE STREET

POINCIANA
TREE

ROW OF PINE TREES

CHONG'S
SHOP

APARTMENTS

APARTMENTS

APARTMENTS

ALLEY

APARTMENTS

APARTMENTS

TO OLD HOUSING DEVELOPMENT

OLD NOI & OLD JAI'S
HOUSE

Primary Characters

Bangkerd: sometimes called Kerd for short, mortician, neighbor

Chong: grocer, called Hia Chong by the neighbors, implying he's of Chinese descent

Dang: tire patcher and bicycle repairman who likes to drink

Jua: the nickname of Thongchai, one of Kampol's best friends and grandson of Old Jai

Kamjon Changsamran: often called Jon, Kampol's baby brother

Kampol Changsamran: also known as Boy

Namfon Changsamran: also called Fon for short, Kampol's mother

Noi: an older boy, neighborhood troublemaker, Kan's son and Gib's younger brother

Oan: the nickname of Prasit Gaewton, one of Kampol's best friends and son of Mon Gaewton

Od: an older neighborhood boy, friends with Rah and Chai

Old Jai: father of Berm, grandfather of Jua, Bow, and twins Gae and Gay

Old Noi: mother of Puang and grandmother of Ampan, Ploy, and Penporn

Phra Soh: monk; the unofficial title *Phra* means "monk"

Somdej: Kampol's deskmate at school

Tia: fisherman who lives in the old housing development

Tongbai: neighbor, married to Gaew

Mrs. Tongjan: landlady; her dog's name is Momo

Wasu Changsamran: Kampol's father, also known by his former name, Ratom; water-truck driver, formerly married to Lim, and now living with her

Bright

Prologue

The mundane has a hard time showing off its quiet allure.

Mrs. Tongjan's cluster of tenement houses is like a lot of other small communities—an image of an era that is just waiting for its time to pass, and to be forgotten. The rows of apartments, built by the small-time landlady, crouch behind an arrogantly large property with vacation bungalows. At the top of the road that runs through the community, a sign—clearly visible during the day and brightly lit at night—grabs the attention of passersby. But it doesn't bear the name of the housing project; it's a sign for the bungalows.

Sometimes empty roads, completely unremarkable, still manage to make people wonder where they might lead. But Mrs. Tongjan's housing development doesn't get even that benefit of the doubt, since the sign at the entrance shuts down further speculation. So, the community is completely cut off from curiosity.

It does happen occasionally that outsiders come along and find the little housing project that hides itself behind the bungalows. As a matter of fact, it happens often, since a number of cars headed for the resort get confused; instead of taking a second turn, to the left this time, they go past the entrance.

It may be the guard's fault, or it could be that the direction arrows are dim compared to the big glowing sign at the entrance from the street, but confused drivers keep following the wall, solid and imposing. They get the hunch that they have gone astray once they find themselves beyond the end of the wall—suddenly on both sides are only thickets of reeds—but the alleyway is too narrow to turn around in. So they have to keep going, unaware that they are about to venture into Mrs. Tongjan's tenement community… First a big house appears on the left, followed by a grocery on the right. Across from the store stands a shady poinciana tree, and next to that an open lot that's perfect for turning around without having to reverse—the driver merely has to rotate as if going around a traffic circle. That nook of an empty lot is framed along two sides with rowhouses that form a right angle. Across the way, next to the store, several more units are lined up along the road. That's all there is to see. It is so unextraordinary that memory can hardly be bothered to register it.

Just once, a little something happened that might be called someone showing "an interest" in this community. Along the shared road, the hotel's wall is not the only one too high to see over on tiptoes. The other side of the street has an even taller one, built on a dirt ridge. Apart from the treetops that peek over the top, passersby can't see any clues as to what the staggering walls keep safe or captive. And from inside Mrs. Tongjan's housing development the only thing visible above the walls is the second floor of a grand house, appearing as if floating in heaven. But the view is of the back of the house; the front faces the main road. One evening, people spotted something on top of the soaring roof of that house. Even from a distance, the figure could be discerned as that of a woman. Some of the children waved to her—it was the first time they had seen a person from that ethereal house. The woman waved back. She was watching them, too. Three days in a row, she climbed up onto the roof and watched the little community in the light of dusk. The children waved to her each day, and she waved back each day. There: a signal that at least one person cared to look at this community, even if from afar.

The woman sat on the roof, under the colors and light of the evening hours. No one ever saw her leave because she stayed perched there until she was swallowed by the dark. No one knows if she slipped off the roof or if she jumped.

She was too far away for anyone to be able to infer anything about the cause of her death, but, it was thought, the last thing she saw before darkness spread a shroud over her life was Mrs. Tongjan's neighborhood. What had she hoped to see over the towering wall? What made her decide to climb onto the roof? Was she trying to see some different view of the world and some people unlike her? And what drew her eye, looking down from up there? In the twilight, the world down below her—as common as it is—probably thrilled her immensely. Perhaps she heard the sounds of children laughing or crying sometimes, of people fighting, of pickup trucks and motorcycles accelerating along the road or in the dirt lot; perhaps she noticed the white roofs—slapped together—of the tenement houses, five rows altogether; a big, handsome home at the front of the development; and another large house, so rundown as to seem abandoned, all the way at the rear.

In a moment of twilit contemplation, she probably found that the ordinary scene before her eyes concealed something of interest beneath its surface, and so she yearned to see it, to touch it, to reach out her hand and feel it, to lean her ear to its heart and listen.... To discover what kind of beings made those faraway noises.

Monopoly

Kampol Changsamran, a five-year-old boy, was hanging out in front of Mrs. Tongjan's tenement houses. His father had told him to wait: "You stay here. I'm taking your brother over to Grandma's. I'll be back in a bit." Hearing these last three words, Kampol didn't dare wander, worried that his father wouldn't spot him when he got back, so he just paced back and forth, keeping an eye on the curve where the road came into the neighborhood.

Something went down at his house a few days ago. His parents had gotten into a nasty fight, and all the neighbors knew it from all the yelling. His mother hurled the fan, breaking its neck. His father flung the kettle over her head, launching it out the window. His mom had left, but later, when night had fallen, she rolled up in a pickup truck, parked in front of the house, and loaded it with stuff until the house was nearly bare. She left on a motorbike, riding ahead as a driver in the pickup truck crawled along behind her. His father watched, arms akimbo, head nodding slightly. Kampol's brother, two months shy of his first birthday, was screaming inside the house.

Kampol waited for his father in front of their unit, the

keys to which they had already surrendered to the landlady. He stood there, sulking, two bags full of his clothing lying next to him on the ground. At midday the neighbor from next door—her name was Aoi, she was the wife of a motor-bike cabbie—called him over, scooped some rice onto a plate, and fed him, questioning him nonstop.

Grown-ups tend to assume that kids live in a different world. In Mrs. Tongjan's neighborhood, there were plenty of people with spare time. The rowhouses formed a little square, with a good shady spot to sit under the poinciana tree—and the vantage point from there was perfect for observing all kinds of things. Importantly, the customers from the grocery situated at a slight diagonal across the way, routinely stopped to exchange a few words with the people gathered under the poinciana. Kampol was grilled about his parents. He recounted the incident over and over again. Some people walked up to him; some waved him over. Another neighbor, On, had given him money to buy a treat and he was called over to the poin-ciana by six or seven adults as he walked back from the store.

"Where'd your papa go, Boy?" Kampol didn't have a nick-name. Everyone just called him "Boy," like his father did.

"He took my brother to Grandma's," he answered.

"What about you? Why didn't he take you?"

"He's coming back to get me soon, to go stay with him at the plant," he replied, as he had when others had asked him the same question.

And where'd your mama go? What were they fighting about, do you know? Did your mama say who she was going to stay with? Do they fight a lot? Is your brother breastfed? Why didn't your mama take you with her? You poor thing, with parents like those… This one isn't his dad's fault, his mama had an affair. But that's karma—his father abandoned two or three wives already.

Kampol held his snack woodenly, eyes glazed over as he stood listening to one person here and another person there discuss his family. He got fed up and hung his head. He missed his father, and he couldn't help daydreaming about having a new home; he was exhausted. In truth, Kampol didn't know much—he just told the people what he'd seen. The more questions he answered, the more he came to know about his parents in the process. He grew irritated and indignant when some of the adults suggested his father might have abandoned him and taken his brother, Jon, or Kamjon, to go live somewhere else. Some of them thought his mother should come to bring him to live with her. "With two kids, you have to split the burden. Since his father took the younger one, he probably meant to leave the older one for the mother." Kampol's feelings were hurt, but he refused to believe them. He resented them. He quit paying attention and craned his neck to check the road instead, keeping his eyes firmly on it.

The group under the poinciana began to disperse once they'd had their fill of the discussion. But one woman reignited it. She had been going to buy fish sauce and stopped by. "I felt bad seeing him like this, so at lunchtime I called him over and gave him something to eat." She shot the kid a look of compassion, her remark putting the other adults on the spot. It was his neighbor Aoi.

"Well…I saw him sitting there staring at his bags so sadly, and I gave him money to get a snack…look there, he hasn't even eaten it yet," On, the wife of a department-store security guard, said.

Everyone fell silent. Nobody had ever thought of acting so generously before. The wave of pity had created an intense wind that stirred a number of people.

Dum, who patched tires, said loudly: "Yeah, I feel really

sorry for him." He called out, "Boy, you can stay at my place tonight if your papa still hasn't come back." Then he turned to the person next to him and said, "He's just a little kid—there's plenty of room to sleep at my place."

Kampol declined without a word, his eyes still stuck on Dum. He wasn't going to have to spend the night at anybody else's house because his father was going to come for him. Tongbai got up and went over to grab the child's hand. "C'mon, Boy…come eat dinner first. Your papa isn't going to show up anytime soon." In a daze, Kampol was tugged along. He wasn't hungry and didn't want to go anywhere with anyone. He worried that his father wouldn't be able to find him when he got back. As the others watched them go, the consensus among the crowd was that Tongbai's behavior was in poor taste. "She's showing off," they said.

At five o'clock that evening, Tongbai was in the kitchen, and the rice in the pot wasn't cooked. Kampol, who was sitting in a funk by his pile of bags, was led into a house of another neighbor. She stuck a plate of rice topped with an omelet in front of his face. It smelled amazing. When the neighbor wasn't paying attention, though, Kampol took his plate outside, back to the spot where he had left his bags. He kept an eye on the bend in the road, where he would first see his father when he returned. Tears welled up and his lips began to quiver. A moment later, Tongbai poked her head out of her door, calling to him. When she saw the plate in his hand, she came over to inspect it.

"Where'd you get the food?"

"Aunt Keow."

Tongbai went back to her house and slammed the door.

At the end of the workday, the road into the housing development started to fill with people and vehicles. Children came back from school; workers made their way home. In the past half hour, Kampol had managed to take only two bites of food. His eyes were moist, he sniffled and whimpered. As people passed by, asking, he would reply that his father hadn't come yet, but would soon. The more he repeated it, the harder he cried. A lot of people came over to console him. "Your grandma's is a long way away. He'll probably be back really late." "If he can't get a ride back, he'll probably have to spend the night." "Don't cry. If he doesn't come back tonight you can stay at my place." "Hey, I already said he could stay with me…"

The sky grew darker. Kampol was taken to the grocery, where treats were put before him to get him to stop crying. His bags were next to him. He continued to sob. Sympathetic adults stood around, forming a crowd in the front of the store, as if he were a problem they had to help resolve. Most of them had something to say about what had put the child in this predicament. His mother shouldn't have had an affair. His father shouldn't have hit her. His mother shouldn't have run off just to save her own skin. Why would his father leave with just the baby? Kampol was bleary-eyed. His sniffling turned into hiccups and he fell asleep like that, hiccupping, in somebody's arms. Dum carried Kampol's bags to his place, but when he returned, the child was gone. An older woman named Rampeuy, who had comforted Kampol until he fell asleep, had carried him to her place. With more than ten pairs of eyes looking on, she proudly went to look after the child's sleeping arrangements.

Late that night, Kampol began screeching. It jolted the neighborhood awake. Kampol got up from the mattress and felt his way in the dark. When the people in the house who had gotten up switched on the lights, Kampol made a dash for the door, flinging it wide and running outside. He called out to his father, his voice echoing down the street. Neighbors turned their lights on and opened their windows. Some cracked their doors and stuck their faces out, trying to see what was going on. Kampol ran down the street, heading for the front of the housing development. Rampeuy caught up to him, grabbed him by the arms, and sat him down. She consoled him for a long time, and then shepherded him back to her home. In the calm of the night, his whimpering cry could be heard throughout the neighborhood.

Early in the morning, Kampol left the house where he had spent the night. He staggered over to the grocery store, looking for his bags. He then just stood there quietly until the shopkeeper turned and saw him.

"Have you seen my papa yet, Hia Chong?" Kampol asked.

"I haven't seen him," Chong said, hands on his hips, looking at Kampol.

"My bags are gone. They were right here yesterday." Kampol pointed to the spot.

"Someone's probably holding on to them for you. They'll bring them back in a bit. Just sit down and wait."

A couple of minutes later, Dum carried the two bags into the store, put them down next to Kampol, bought a pack of cigarettes, and left for home. A long succession of other people came in to do their shopping, and each one seemed to ask Kampol, "Your papa's not back?" Kampol gave no answer, but the grown-ups didn't press him to say any more. They had started getting used to the Kampol situation, and it was losing its novelty. But that wasn't the case among the kids, some of whom were his classmates. It was Saturday and the kids were home, so his friends shared gossip from school with him. Kampol had a dance partner he'd been rehearsing with for weeks. The day before had been the day of the school fair, but Kampol hadn't gone to school.

"She was right in the front. But when she found out you weren't coming, she refused to dance. She wanted to get off the stage. Her parents clung to the front of the stage, telling her, 'Dance, Sweetie, dance… You can just dance alone… I want to see you dance.' Eventually she did dance. When it got to the part where you were supposed to lock arms and twirl, she just stood there, looking around confused, and then she started bawling. And she was wearing a fancy red skirt, and high heels too. Her mama had to go up and carry her off, and on top of all of it she dropped her shoes. She was full-on shrieking. It was hilarious. Tons of people were watching. Everyone was like, 'You poor thing!'

"After the dancing there were games, with toys and treats for prizes, and there was free ice cream! The bigger kids did some comedy skits on the stage, and the teachers put on a play. Our own Mr. Sanya played a kindergartner with pigtails." Kampol's friend was in stitches as he recounted the story. Without realizing it, Kampol had forgotten about his father. Picturing the dance made him laugh hard with his classmate. His friend's name was Prasit, but Kampol called him by his nickname: Oan.

Oan heard his mother calling in the distance and ran off toward home. But he came back in a flash with a plate of food in his hand. They took turns having bites with the one spoon. They were having fun and their shared lunch was tasty. When the food ran out, Oan ran back for seconds. Then the two of them had a heart-to-heart about Kampol's father while they sat watching TV in the grocery.

At eleven o'clock the crew under the poinciana tree yelled to Kampol…his father was back. The child leaped into the street, wailing and crying his father's name. He ran toward him as if it were the climax of a movie. All eyes were on them, but the image wasn't flawless because there was an extra in the shot—Oan, chasing behind.

His father reeked. The son reeked, too. They were wearing the same clothes as when they had parted. Father and son flew headlong into each other.

"Have you eaten anything?" his father asked.

"He ate," Oan answered for him. "We ate breakfast together this morning."

"How about yesterday? Did you get anything to eat?"

Kampol nodded.

"Who fed you?"

"For lunch, Aunt Aoi had me over to eat. For dinner, Aunt Tongbai was going to have me eat at her place, but the rice wasn't done so Aunt Keow gave me some food."

"Good. Where'd you sleep last night?"

Kampol made a face, thinking… "At Aunt Peuy's."

"Good, that's good. That's what I figured. Now come here…over here."

The father and son evaded people's prying eyes by disappearing around the corner of a wall. Oan stubbornly followed them, but they didn't pay him any mind.

"Listen, I still can't find a place. I've been sleeping in the cab of the truck at night. You've got to stay here another day or two; then I'll come get you and take you to our new home."

Kampol, his face pinched, shook his head. "I'm coming with you. I'll sleep in the truck's cab, too!"

"You can't… You're better off here—there are compassionate people who'll help you. You'll find a place to eat and sleep. It's just two more days. Do you understand?"

Kampol didn't understand. He could only cry and cling

tightly to his father. But his friend, Oan, understood. His eyes lit up as he imagined the fun they were going to have.

"Come sleep over at my place," Oan told him. "Tell him to stay with me." He looked at Kampol's father.

The man only saw Oan now. "What's your name? Whose kid are you?"

"I'm Oan, Mon's son."

"Mon, the seamstress? Good. Oan, get your parents to let your friend stay over for a couple of nights, all right? And when it's time to eat, get him then, too. And let everybody know that I'm leaving Boy here for a couple of days, and ask them to help look after him, you understand?"

Excited and proud, Oan enthusiastically accepted.

"Boy…your papa's going through a rough time. You've got to help me out. If you can't be strong, then we'll be in a real mess. I'm going to work both the day and night shifts and ask the boss if I can stay in the boarding room at the plant. It's only two days. Monday evening, I'll come back to get you. Stay here with your friend, all right? Have fun. OK, I'm going. Don't cry. Aren't you embarrassed to cry in front of your friend? OK…I'm off."

Kampol's father had come—and left—as if it were a dream. The neighbors hadn't even gotten a chance to get a good look at him yet. When they saw the son walking back alone, the group under the poinciana waved him over. They crowded around and pummeled him with questions. Kampol barely answered, but Oan told them everything.

So it was finally clear and everybody understood: Kampol was no longer just a neighborhood kid they saw around; he had become everybody's burden.

"It's no big deal," someone said, "it's only two days. Dum, you have plenty of room, don't you?"

Dum was caught off guard, stricken momentarily mute, but eventually he managed to say, "Two days aren't a problem. But what if his father bails for good? What if he takes the opportunity to ditch him? Then what are we going to do? I can't take that on. Find someone else. Who was it that let him spend the night yesterday?"

"It hasn't even been a minute, and you're already talking like this," Rampeuy said. "His father asked everybody to pitch in, not for one person to take on the responsibility alone. I helped out last night. Who'll volunteer for tonight if Dum won't?"

"But Dum has a point. What if his father bails?"

"We'll deal with that when it happens."

"What's wrong with planning ahead?"

"Yeah, you all keep planning... I've got work to do. I'm leaving."

"See? Everybody's already hightailing it out of here. Look at all your sorry little faces. Who's got a big enough heart to give a boy a place to eat and sleep?"

Oan watched the scene unfold, completely baffled. He tried to get a word in but couldn't.

Tongbai finally said, "Fine, lunch today at my place. I'll do dinner, too, if no one else is going to feed him."

"Ha! 'If no one's going to feed him,'" somebody fumed. "It's just a plate of food... There's no need to throw a cheap shot at us."

"Yeah, if you're going to talk like that, why don't you just take him in yourself?"

"Because it's none of my damn business," Tongbai replied. "If he were my relative, that'd be another thing. If somebody really feels like showing off their compassion I say go ahead."

"What did you say? Who's showing off?"

"All of you."

"Whoa there…"

Noon approached as they fought. Kampol and Oan stood on the sideline, riveted. The performers outnumbered the audience, and as the yelling and insults grew more explosive it became impossible to make out the words. Eventually, a jumble of blows ensued and when no one made an attempt to untangle the fight, it just went on, unrelenting for a long time, as everyone divided onto one side or the other. Chong, the grocer, finally couldn't bear watching any longer from his store. He ran over, whispered something to Kampol and Oan, then ran back to his grocery.

"The police are coming!" the kids screamed. "Police! Police!"

It worked pretty well. Several people backed away, pulling other members of their crew with them. Worn out as they were, they still had enough energy to curse at each other awhile before they scattered, everyone going back to their own home.

Kampol and Oan went over and gave a report to Chong about the fight. Chong tried to give them his full attention but still had a hard time piecing the plot together. All he understood was that they had been arguing about Kampol, arguing about something like who would get to look after the boy.

"But Boy's sleeping over at my place anyway," Oan said. "His dad told him to stay with me…I tried to tell them but they wouldn't listen. They just kept arguing. Someone said something about being a show-off, and someone else said, 'Who are you calling a show-off?' And then, boom, fists flying."

The two boys took Kampol's bags over to Oan's house.

When they poked their heads in, they saw Oan's mother sleeping, folded over the sewing machine. Across the room, a wardrobe blocked the view of his parents' bed. The mattress on the ground, where Oan slept, was cordoned off by a dark blue curtain. Their food cupboard backed up to one side of the mattress. The kids put the bags down next to Oan's bed and went into the kitchen to look for something to eat. They made two plates with rice and some leftovers from breakfast. Once full, they spent some time jumping on the mattress, going over who was fighting with whom and what move they were using. Then they played Monopoly until they fell asleep.

Oan's mother, Mon, woke up in a panic at three in the afternoon. She had to resume working, but stumbled into the kitchen area first. She didn't even notice the two kids asleep on the mattress. There was nothing left in the kitchen—the rice pot was empty and the cupboard was cleaned out. She stood for a moment, dazed, then lit the gas stove, poured some water in the kettle, and placed it over the flame. Only when she stepped out of the kitchen area did she catch sight of her son and the other boy sprawled out, sleeping. She looked at them for a quick second but then turned away; she was in a bind and didn't have time to pay attention to anything else. She went over to the grocery, bought a pack of instant noodles, then hurried back and dealt with her lunch—all in just fifteen minutes. Then she took up her seat at the sewing machine again, foot pumping, hands pressing, lips pursed, brow furrowed, and eyes focused as the machine whirred.

Just before five o'clock that afternoon, Mon arranged the clothes into their separate bags and hustled out of the house. Her husband had another sewing machine set up in front of the bank in the market. They patched and mended all kinds of garments. Mon took some of the clothes that people dropped off with her husband, worked on them at home, and then brought them back at pickup time. This afternoon, she was so frantic that her hands shook, but she was too late. Two customers had shown up early for their clothes. Oan's father had asked them to wait a couple of minutes, but they couldn't stay. They made new appointments to pick up their clothes the following day.

Mon sighed and sat down, deflated. "We're out of money," she said.

"Yeah, yeah, I know. But two more people are supposed to pick up today. They'll probably be here in a bit."

The couple slowly packed up. They carried the sewing machine over to leave it in the stir-fry-and-curry joint next to the bank for the night and returned to wait for the customers.

"It's almost six," Mon said.

"Yeah…let's wait a little more."

"Give me fifty and I'll go get food."

"Where am I supposed to get fifty baht? Go home and get the rice ready. I'll pick up something to go with it and be home in a bit."

When Mon got home, she saw that they were out of rice, too. She went outside and sat in front of the house, sighing.

Oan dashed over. "Mama, can I have money for some candy?" He had told Kampol he would treat.

"Go take a shower right now," she scolded. "And make sure you get the grime behind your ears. Go!"

Oan and Kampol showered together, playing to their hearts' content before emerging from the bathroom—they then smeared their faces white with baby powder. They went into the kitchen and looked in the rice pot. Seeing no rice, they turned and opened the food cupboard—nothing. The used bowls and plates from their lunch were still soaking in the tub out back. Oan ran to the front of the house.

"Mama, can we cook some rice?"

"Come here," his mother called him over. "Go to Hia Chong's shop. Tell him your mama wants to buy a bag of rice."

Oan nodded, but then she remembered that they had nothing to eat the rice with.

"Wait, Oan, come back here first. Ask Hia Chong for two packs of Mama noodles, too. Let's have instant noodles tonight."

"Can we get a pack for my friend?"

As soon as his mother nodded, the two ran off at full speed to Chong's shop.

At the store, Dum was bargaining with Chong, but unsuccessfully. Chong only shook his head, leaving Dum to grumble as he went to attend to other customers. One customer was asking to get fish sauce and eggs on credit. When he heard Chong agree, Dum threw even more of a tantrum. He was making a lot of noise, slurring his words and getting tongue-tied, stumbling and swaying as he tried to walk.

"C'mon, one last bottle," Dum begged, following Chong, who had gone toward the back to grab something for a customer.

"Enough, Dum. I can't give you another one," Chong said.

"Just one more, c'mon."

"It's already been two bottles today. I said enough is enough. You still owe me two hundred from before, plus over a hundred just today…Wait, what are you doing? You can't just grab… Give it back. If you're going to act like this, I'm going to have to quit playing nice."

"C'mon, just this one. You let other people put things on their tabs…"

"Hey kids, what would you two like?"

"Mama sent me for a bag of rice and three packs of Mama, on her tab."

Chong smiled drably, shaking his head. He was fed up, but obliged, turning to fetch the stuff for them. Rice he had, but the Mama noodles were out.

"Tell your mother this is the last time. She's got to settle up her tab before I'll let her add more."

"Look at that…you even let kids buy on credit. I just want one more bottle."

Chong perused the list of accounts in his ledger and sighed a number of times. He'd been in a good mood this morning. Given all the unpaid balances, he had made a resolution that he wouldn't give out any liquor, beer, or cigarettes on credit for the day—he would allow only the necessities. And he got to allow a lot of necessities: it seemed like every wallet in the neighborhood was thin. He'd moved a fair amount of inventory, but the sum of money in the register was meager. Still, he'd mostly kept up his resolution: he let every customer buy on credit, except for liquor, beer, and cigarettes. Alas, he had already succumbed to Dum's doggedness.

Dum had been stationed in front of the grocery for over an hour. He was fuming, bitter because during the confusion of the brawl—when nobody could tell who was who—someone had yanked a fistful of hair out of his head. The middle of his crown, which used to have a scattering of hair still attached, was now just bare, reddish scalp. He successfully pleaded his case for whiskey on credit by displaying his sore head to Chong, telling him how he probably wouldn't be able to sleep that night if he didn't have a little alcohol to soothe his pain. Chong gave in, handed him a bottle, and told him to go home. Less than an hour later, though, Dum was back again. He ranted until Chong caved and let him have another bottle.

With his resolution twice broken, Chong was in no mood to smile or kid around with anyone. When Dum showed his face for the third time, he started a mental countdown to the moment he would throw him out of the store. But when his eyes fell on Dum's raw head, he contained himself. Everyone in the neighborhood had been having a pretty rough day.

As for Tongbai, she went home still steaming about the scuffle and refused to cook or clean. When her husband came home, she had another round of arguing. Her husband announced that he wouldn't give her any money, so she declared that she wouldn't feed him. In the end, her husband ran over to the grocery to buy a pack of Mama noodles, and a minute later she followed to get some Mama for herself on credit. And Tongbai and her husband weren't the only ones to argue that night. The big fight set off at least two other family spats, which could be heard all the way down to the store.

"He's out of instant noodles," Oan told his mother.

Mon sighed. "Go back again. Get ten baht worth of eggs."

"Hia Chong said before you get anything more on credit, the old tab's got to be paid off."

Mon slipped into the house without bothering to listen to the end. After she made the rice, she came back out and sat, chin on palm, as before. The sky was losing its light. All her hope depended on her husband. After a while, though, another solution dawned on her. She went inside to rummage through the bag of clothes on the table. There was a pair of pants from a customer who lived close by. She could change the zipper in a heartbeat. Oan went into the kitchen, but came back out again to remind his mother that there was nothing to eat, only rice.

"Yeah, hold on…don't go anywhere. In a bit, I'll need you to go and deliver these pants for me."

Fifteen minutes later she was done. Visibly relieved, she put the pants in a bag.

"Take this to Aunt Tongbai. Tell her it's twenty baht. And on your way back, get ten baht of eggs."

The kids ran out. A short while later they came back and Oan told his mother, "Aunt Tongbai and her husband are fighting. She told him, 'Give me twenty for the zipper. That time you needed your pants patched, I paid for it.' Her husband said back to her, 'Give you twenty? How about I give you a kick instead?' So Aunt Tongbai told us, 'You two go back home now. I'll come and pay your mama in a bit.'"

Mon didn't say anything. She could only switch the hand that was propping her chin, from the left to the right.

Oan began to worry that they wouldn't have anything for his friend to eat. The two sat down, limp, next to Mon.

"If my papa were here, we could buy some food on credit no problem because my papa's already paid off everything he owes," Kampol said.

"I don't owe anything *personally*, but I'm scared to go," Oan said.

"Me neither. Should we give it a try?" Kampol said, hoping to rally his friend. "We can tell Hia Chong that my papa's going to pay on Monday."

"Sure, let's give it a go. But you talk."

The two of them got up and shyly made their way to the store. Mon watched them go, her gaze hanging inertly in their direction. Her husband, it was clear, was no longer any hope for her. By now he had probably put his empty stomach in the care of some friend.

It was only seven thirty, but Chong was getting ready to close up the shop. After seeing Dum walk by again, booze in hand, he felt worn out and had lost his will to keep the store open. He wanted the battered day to end swiftly so he could start over with a new one.

The last customers popped up before he locked the gate. Two pairs of gleaming eyes were on him.

Slumping, Chong grabbed four eggs and slipped the bag through the grille.

The children sprinted off, giggling. The sound of them slowly faded.

Masseur

Kampol Changsamran, dark-skinned with large, sad eyes, drifted from one home to another without a regular place to eat or sleep. His family had been tenants in one of the rowhouses, where they'd all lived together—mother, father, and two sons. Several months ago, his mother had started an affair and now she'd run off. His father gave up their apartment because he couldn't afford the rent, and left his baby brother, one year old, at their grandma's. As for Kampol, his father came back to see him once a week, always promising to bring him to their new home. But in the end, he would always ask a neighbor—sometimes this person, sometimes that person—to keep an eye on his son, and Kampol was becoming more and more like an orphan with each passing day.

There were a number of children with no parents around to give them pocket money, and even the ones with parents, most of them didn't receive allowances anyway. Because of that, the kids, regardless of what they were doing, were on a constant lookout for an opportunity to earn themselves some cash.

One day, a large man named Dang, coming home from a day of selling curries and stir-fries out of his pickup truck, beckoned for Kampol to come over to his house. Kampol's friends simply assumed that Dang was going to feed him. But Kampol didn't reemerge from Dang's home for over two hours.

"What were you doing in there, Boy?"

Kampol smiled like he had something up his sleeve but didn't say anything. He kept one hand in his shorts pocket, the twenty-baht note held tight in his fist. It took a great deal of willpower, but he refused to take the money out and buy a snack in front of his friends.

The next day, when he spotted Dang's pickup truck at the same time, Kampol sprinted over without waiting to be summoned. It was only an hour—ten baht. Kampol was dreaming: he was going to be rich! Some days he got ten, some days twenty, but if it continued like that every day, he was going to have enough saved up for a new house. But it was important that it remain a secret. If Oan, Noi, Jua, or anyone else found out, his dream would be snuffed like a blown candle.

Kampol carried out his mission furtively and alone. He decided to increase his vigilance by keeping his distance from the others. When that time of day neared, he disappeared without a trace.

One day, at three thirty in the afternoon, Dang's truck rolled in, his big wife sound asleep in the passenger seat. Dang stopped the vehicle and scanned the group of kids shooting marbles. He asked about Kampol, but everyone shook their head.

"In that case, one of you will do. Come over to my house—but just one person."

The children hesitated. "What for?"

"To walk on my back for me. I'll give you ten baht an hour."

"I'll go!… Me! Me!" The children fought to raise their hands, screaming over one another.

No one was willing to back down, all of them chasing after Dang's truck, forming a tail right behind it.

At that point, Kampol, who had been crouched down next to Dang's gardenia bush, stood up. At first he'd been scared by all the ruckus, but then his outrage won out. He'd made an effort to come wait for Dang in front of his house, but the tactic had proven wrong. Kicking dust, Kampol walked over to Chong's store, starting to doubt whether saving his money for a house was a good idea.

"There's no need to fight," Dang was telling the kids. "I'll give you each a tryout. Whoever gives the best service will get to be my regular masseur."

Everyone went for broke. One kid went five minutes longer than everybody else, then another kid went ten minutes longer. They invented all kinds of moves, with their hands, feet, and even knees all thrown in. Dang, with his massive build, felt fantastic with the kids doing gymnastics on his back, but his wife wasn't pleased: As one kid was giving a massage, the others were sticking their noses through the window and making a lot of noise. She and her husband had to get up every day at three a.m. to go shopping for ingredients, and then they sold the food they cooked until three in the afternoon. Only then could they come home and rest. Beyond exhausted though she was, just like every day, she couldn't sleep with all the noise coming from the children, so eventually…

Kampol was munching on something. His pockets were empty now. He chewed listlessly, feeling obviously down. From a distance, he saw his usual crew, bunched up at Dang's window, suddenly burst apart and run away wildly. The lady they called Aunt Fatty was standing in front of her house, hands on her hips.

"How's a person supposed to sleep?" she shrilled. "All that yapping! Enough is enough. From now on, I'll do the damn massages myself."

Three days later, Kampol ran into Dang. "Do you feel like a massage?"

Dang paused, letting the gears in his head turn a little. Then he beckoned Kampol to come closer.

"Let me teach you a little trick," he whispered. "You have to be as quiet as possible. Don't let anybody else find out under any circumstance, you understand? Do you see the gardenia bush in front of my house? At three thirty, go hide there—get real low. Don't let anyone see you. It'll be our little secret. You can start tomorrow, and I'll let you know when the next time after that will be."

Kampol lit up, dreaming big dreams.

Hunger Might Make a Person...

Hunger makes you feel as if you *have* to fill your belly. With the right timing, it makes any food taste better. But left too long, it can turn a person into a thief, or even a killer; a person might be willing to destroy for a measly chicken drumstick. Vagrants are well acquainted with hunger. It starts as an endless suffering, but then it becomes a friend, a close companion you know well, one that rarely leaves your side.

"C'mon now, come and eat." In the first days after he was left behind, all the neighbors were worried about Kampol going hungry. From sunup to sundown, voices echoed through the neighborhood, calling him to come and eat.

But later, Kampol often went without lunch, the midday hours slipping by undisturbed. He frequently lost track of time playing, but it was really because the adults forgot to yell for him, or if they didn't forget, they each assumed another neighbor had the kid covered for the day. Kampol still hadn't gotten to know real hunger, though, because dinner would always come to the rescue in time.

The day Kampol was first besieged by real hunger, he got woken up early in the morning at the home of a woman who worked in a factory, Aoi. The day before, Aoi's husband, Chart, had been feeling generous and had invited Kampol over for dinner, and that evening they had put together a place for him to sleep as well. People had begun to observe this routine almost as a tradition: wherever Kampol ate dinner, he spent the night, followed the next morning by breakfast.

But at Aoi and Chart's, there was never any breakfast. By six forty-five at the latest, Aoi had to be out the door to catch the factory bus, which picked her up along the side of the main road. She picked up her breakfast from the food stall right outside the plant. Chart left the house even earlier. A motorbike-taxi driver, he had to whizz off to his stand by about six a.m. He counted on the food cart that came by at seven to get something to fill his stomach.

Because of that, Kampol, still half asleep, ended up sitting outside, slumped over, bleary-eyed and feeling exposed in the damp and cool morning air. The aroma of fried fish from one kitchen or another grazed his nose, and without realizing it, he inhaled deeply. In his mind, he saw a massive fried fish, steaming on a plate. But once the smell vanished, he forgot all about it. He kept himself entertained by watching what was going on in the neighborhood, which was quickly waking up: children were going to school, adults headed to work. The only slowpokes were the security guards coming home after their night shifts. They walked as if they couldn't care less how much time it took to get where they were going. Kampol made it through the morning without breakfast having made it into him.

Penporn, Old Noi's youngest grandchild, who was mentally disabled, and Jua, Old Jai's grandson, who had a bad limp, didn't go to school, so they came and found Kampol to go play as usual. They had their regular spot, which was under the rukam tree behind Mrs. Tongjan's large house. At noon his two friends ran home for lunch, leaving Kampol to fend for himself. Feeling like he had no energy left, he lolled on the ground. He was hungry but he didn't understand hunger so he thought he was sick and that was why he didn't feel like standing up or moving. A faint smell of food drifted over to him from Mrs. Tongjan's house. As he inhaled, his mind wandered back to the imaginary fried fish from that morning, and he again dreamed he saw that fish on a plate. He'd fallen asleep, depleted.

In his dream, his father carried the plate over and put it down in front of him. The fish was enormous, golden, and fragrant. But when he went to scoop some meat with his spoon, the fish, though already fried, flapped off the plate. He chased after it; the fish kept flapping away. Finally, he almost caught it, but he was still too slow: a giant cat pounced on the fish and made off with it. Kampol broke down in tears.

Through the afternoon, Kampol went in and out of sleep beneath the rukam tree. By the time he got up, the sun was already hanging low. He staggered as he stood up, his cheeks still tear-stained. While the cook at Mrs. Tongjan's was busy seasoning her delicacies, Kampol wandered to the window, clenching his stomach as he exhaled. His eyes just cleared the windowsill; he peered at the dishes arrayed on the kitchen table and the ones still being finished on the stove. He felt pools of saliva collect in the pockets of his cheeks; he swallowed them down. Oh, why had there been no usual holler today, the one that had grown almost banal, even to him: "C'mon now, come and eat"? But such an invitation had never come from Mrs. Tongjan's house, and he was afraid of making a sound, so all he did was stand there and ogle, which he did for a while, until everything was ready to go, all the food carried out, nothing left in the kitchen for him to feast on with his eyes.

Kampol walked back toward the rows of tenement houses without anybody noticing him. In a bit of a daze, he stumbled to the daybed that sat under the poinciana tree across from Chong's shop. The sky was about to lose its light. Curled up on the daybed, Kampol looked like a shadow, or perhaps an empty pile of clothes. How strange that no one had thought of him today. Even the friends he normally played with were nowhere to be found.

In hunger, he fell asleep. It was the swarm of mosquitoes around him that ended up content and full.

As Chong was closing up shop, the scraping of his metal gate woke Kampol up. He started crying when he opened his eyes to total darkness. Chong froze, listening… and then he became the first and only person that day to think of the boy.

Chong walked over to Kampol, led him back to the store, and had him sit down. All the loneliness in the world ganged up on him, beating him mercilessly. He sobbed hard. Chong spent a long time consoling him, but to no avail. In the end, when Kampol shook his head in response to his question, Chong's heart broke: not a morsel had gotten into the boy's stomach all day. Chong quickly brought warm milk and sliced bread with jam, but they made Kampol cry even harder: seeing the food, he realized for the first time that this was what real hunger felt like. Chong went back into the kitchen and started frying rice. Kampol was famished, but there was even more sadness in him than hunger.

When the fried rice was added to the spread, the level in the milk glass hadn't gone down at all, and the jam-smeared bread flaunted its tastiness in vain. Chong thought, standing with his hands on his hips: Just look at the boy. You'd expect him, starved as he is, to scarf all that down until he nearly choked. He must be so sad—even his hunger is secondary. Despite the fact that his body's suffering, his mind still prevails… And the boy's only five… Then Chong thought of something, so he ran upstairs. He grabbed a book from the shelf, hurried back down, and sat across from Kampol. "Listen, the poem's called 'Toy on Target.'" He began reading in a crisp voice:

> 1
> *Dropping*
> *toys*
> *instead of bombs*
> *for the Festival of the Children*
>
> *that*
> *said the market researchers*
> *will undoubtedly make*
> *an impression*
>
> *It has made*
> *a great*
> *impression*
> *on the whole world*

Kampol listened, confounded, but he had stopped sniveling.

> 2
> *If the airplane*
> *had dropped the toys*
> *a fortnight ago*
> *and only now the bombs*

my two children
thanks to your kindness
would have had something to play with
for those two weeks

"Did the plane drop toys?" Kampol asked.

Chong gave him a hint of a smile and said, "Yes, the plane came and dropped toys for the children... Here, have some of this milk and I'll tell you about it... They'd dropped bombs first, but then two weeks later..."

Kampol finished his milk and started on the bread. He was eating happily until he reached for the fried rice, at which point his large eyes welled up again. Unconsciously, he put the spoon down.

"They both died?"

"Yes, both of them," Chong said quietly, looking at Kampol and the abandoned fried rice uneasily.

Kampol's eyes had a distant look to them, and tears poured out.

Chong quickly closed the book and tiptoed upstairs to put it back.

Winning Numbers

Twice a month on lottery day, Noi, watching the scene around Mrs. Tongjan's neighborhood, wanted to kick himself. Back when he'd lived at the market, he used to run around hawking newspapers, which had the results printed on the back page, at various intersections. The papers were five baht each: the printing house got three, he got two.

"I used to sell out fifty copies in under an hour—an easy hundred baht."

Kampol, Oan, and Jua were in awe. Noi was a bit of a ringleader, and was a few years older. They wanted to move to the market, too, but Noi had another idea.

"If we could get someone to print sheets with the results, we could just sell them here."

"Who could we get to print them? Maybe I could get my mama to do it?" Oan suggested.

"No, we need someone with their own printing press."

"Couldn't you just write them out by hand?" Kampol asked.

"Ha! Dummy, think about how long it would take to write out each sheet," Noi said, and then he got up and walked away, feeling hopeless.

Kampol, Oan, and Jua started scheming up ways to sell lists of the winning lottery numbers.

Jua's mother worked at a paper-baling plant. When Jua asked, she started bringing home big booklets of job application forms where each page was perforated and the backs of the forms were blank. Chong dug out a couple of sheets of carbon paper for them and taught them how to use them. He also lent them his radio so they could listen to the drawings, and let them use the kitchen area in the back of the shop for their operation. The three of them didn't say a word about it to anyone. Not even Noi knew about it.

On the first and the sixteenth of every month, in the morning the adults ran around exuberantly. They were flush with money and hope was high. On those mornings, if the children misbehaved, they were graciously forgiven. In small waves, men and women arrived on their bikes, with some parking in front of the grocery and some under the poinciana tree. The lottery display case would be folded open, and people would huddle around it. Rampeuy, the nanny who hadn't had a child to watch for almost a year now, would jump on her bicycle and run the bets for the dealer. She only worked on the first and the sixteenth, but she made more money on those two days than she did looking after kids for a whole month.

That afternoon, the television at the grocery was invariably tuned to the channel that broadcast the national lottery draw. People from the neighborhood gathered, chatting in little groups, everyone waiting to hear the special final digits and the grand prize, the only numbers relevant to the underground lottery.

Kampol and Oan were on recording duty as the radio announced the winning numbers. Jua, with his terrible handwriting, was assigned to be the seller. Besides, with his bad leg the grown-ups would be more inclined to pity him and buy a sheet from him. Each winning number was announced twice. As close as Kampol and Oan tried to listen, *two* sometimes sounded an awful lot like *three*, and *four* was sometimes hard to distinguish from *five*. When one of them missed a number, Jua would go look at what the other one had to try and fill it in.

Immediately after the grand prize numbers were announced, the first two copies were torn from the kids' books. Jua limped out with them in his hand. Kampol and Oan then reinserted the carbon paper and started copying all over again. Jua went around trying to sell the sheets, crying, "Three baht, three baht." The adults looked at him, not entirely convinced he was actually selling something; most of them thought he was just fooling around. But he finally made the sales. Mon, Oan's mother, was their first customer.

Mon had actually been trying to track down Oan to make him deliver some clothes to a customer. But once she found out that her son was making lottery lists for sale, she bought a copy and then delivered the clothes herself. Her purchase sparked other people's interest. Once Jua sold the other sheet, he quickly limped his way back. Four more copies were already ripped out and ready for him. His two friends were giddy with excitement when they saw the money Jua slapped on the table. They both continued their copying in earnest.

By evening, the scene around the neighborhood had turned. It was as if all the energy had been used up in the morning, leaving behind only somber silence. Each lottery cycle, on the first and the sixteenth, there might have been one or two people whose luck permitted them to stay cheerful into the evening. Rampeuy, of course, was an exception, since she was in a good mood only on those two days every month.

Among the sullen who had had their hopes dashed by the underground lottery, some had backup chances to keep their dreams alive if they hadn't yet had a chance to check their state lottery tickets. Jua made the rounds with the results sheets until dusk. At seven that evening, a man whooped—he'd won fifth prize. As soon as he realized his luck, he couldn't run fast enough to the grocery store to put a bottle of whiskey on his tab. It was Dum, the tire patcher and bicycle repairman. He assembled a crew to drink and treated his friends late into the night.

The next day, Dum got ready to go to the market bright and early. He stopped to get cigarettes right as the newspapers were being delivered. Kampol was also at the grocery store early getting himself some crackers. Because Dum still couldn't get over his luck, before he headed off to claim his prize money, he took his lottery ticket out to check it against the newspaper again.

He checked and rechecked but still he didn't have the right numbers. One digit was off.

"What? Did they misprint a number?" Dum squawked, but then he realized that probably wasn't the case. He looked up from the newspaper, his eyes hostile, and growled, "That bastard Jua!"

Kampol jumped.

Hiding Place

One more term and Kampol would have finished first grade, but he never went back to school after he was abandoned. Penporn, the mentally disabled girl, had been sent to school, but one month in, her teacher notified her family that attending was doing her no good, and on top of it she was a burden on her teacher and classmates. So that was the end of Penporn's foray into formal education. Jua, or as his teachers called him, Thongchai, sometimes went to school, sometimes didn't. With his bad leg and the long walk to school, he didn't like making the trip. Another outcast was Noi, who didn't go to school simply because he didn't want to learn. This sorry crew made up Kampol's weekday friends.

On weekends, Mrs. Tongjan's neighborhood was like a playground. When the kids gathered for hide and seek, they always came to exactly fifteen. As they started the game, they made such a cacophony—some of the adults couldn't stand it. But when these grown-ups came out to give them a piece of their mind, they would find the pandemonium had died down. The group would have inevitably dissolved, with the kids having run off to take cover and hide. There would be one lone child standing in the middle of the lot with his or her eyes covered. The adults would just sigh and head back inside their homes.

The kids never gave it much thought: they scattered and hid anywhere that provided cover, be it behind a pickup truck or a door, in a bush or water barrel, up in a tree, or around the back of the rowhouses. It never took long for them all to be discovered, but often the person who was "it" got tagged before all the hiders were found and just had to be "it" again.

One time, a few adults were in a silly mood and asked to play with the kids. Then they felt obliged to show the children that they could come up with the best, most unexpected hiding places. The kids—definitely wanting to hide in the best, most unexpected places—put their faith in the grown-ups. That being the case, a whole bunch of them chased after the adults. They ventured farther than ever before. The parade of hiders even ran past Mrs. Tongjan's house. They came to an abandoned field cluttered with giant reeds. The dried thickets reached higher than their heads. The whole crew of them charged in, shoving the reeds out of the way and crouching down to hide.

The reeds were silent, giving away nothing of the dozen or so children and adults taking refuge among them. But after about ten seconds, a little voice let out a yelp, then the kid responsible for it bolted out.

"Ah! There's a hornet nest in here!" someone squealed.

There was a big rush to get up. The grown-up who'd masterminded the spot hightailed it out of there before anybody, but still wasn't fast enough. He took one in the left temple. The children screamed in the chaos.

Kampol had one hiding place that no one else knew about. He'd once gone off to hide behind the houses. The unit he and his family had lived in was still vacant, even then. Kampol had seen that the back door wasn't all the way shut. He knew immediately that it wasn't locked from the inside, because it always stuck and you had to really slam it into the frame to get the bolt to slide. Mrs. Tongjan must have shown the unit to a potential tenant and opened the back door. But when she went to lock up, she hadn't known the trick and left it a bit open. Kampol knew that door well. He had slipped his little hand underneath it, gripping the bottom edge and yanking on it repeatedly. Before long, the door had swung open. He snuck in and jammed it closed, but not too tight, just enough to get it to stick in the jamb.

Kampol hid in the empty room, or what was still, to him, his home. Once, it had been so full of stuff that there was no space to walk: bed; wardrobe; shoe rack; table with baby bottles and his little brother's things; bedclothes with a red, pink, and green floral pattern; a navy blue and red plaid blanket on the bed; the cushioned mat where his brother used to sleep. Jon crying, struggling with his hands and feet; his mother pacing back and forth, her sarong secured over her chest; his father shaving in front of the mirror.

Kampol, lulled by his memories, dozed off. In his sleep, he kept dreaming. It felt as though he had traveled back in time, and he had been reunited with his whole family again.

When he awoke, his stomach hurt, and he walked groggily into the bathroom out of habit. As he was wobbling toward the toilet, he heard an angry voice:

"Boy, did you sneak into the water tank again? You're going to get hit until you learn your lesson!"

Kampol jumped, his eyes wide. He looked around. The cement water tank was almost all the way full. He had submerged himself in there so many times and hung out, only his head above the water. He hadn't been dreaming. He'd heard his mother scolding him. His father and Jon must be here, too. He dashed out of the bathroom…but the unit was hushed and empty.

Kampol threw the door shut behind him, leaving it as he'd found it. He stepped out into the real world.

"Boy, where the heck did you hide?" Oan asked when they ran into each other. "People quit playing ages ago."

Kampol chuckled but refused to say. He had found the best hiding place: you'd have to travel back in time to discover it. He skipped away joyfully. But then his melancholy caught up to him and his steps grew slow and measured—he didn't know where to go.

Fair Game

The fair at the Zeng Tek Xiang Tung Shrine was held over the course of three nights. Since it was nearby, the folks from Mrs. Tongjan's community grabbed all the kids and headed over for an evening out. Kampol went with Oan and his mother, Mon.

The first thing they had to do was survey the entire fairground. A steady stream of people came in, flowing in one general direction. Parents, worried that they would get separated from their children, gripped their hands tightly. Mon did the same, with Oan on her right and Kampol on her left. Along both sides of the walkway, stands dazzled the eyes with a panoply of mouthwatering treats: marshmallow crepes, coconut pancakes, fried bananas, cotton candy, shaved ices. Next came the toy stalls hawking superhero masks, bright balloons, race cars, dolls…there were even gold and silver fish for sale.

Kampol held the twenty baht in his pocket tight in his fist—Dang had paid him to give him a massage earlier that afternoon—unable to decide what to spend it on: the merry-go-round, the Ferris wheel, or the train that did a loop around the entire fairground. He had his eye on a superhero mask, as did Oan, but Mon forbade them from wasting their money buying toys; only snacks were allowed.

As they drifted away from the vendor stalls, Mon steered the children toward the Chinese-opera theater, but the curtain was still down so they went to peek backstage. The performers, both men and women, were sitting around putting on their makeup. One of them walked by in nothing but an ordinary pair of shorts, but his face was done up in full opera makeup. The boys ogled, following him as he went to buy himself some grilled squid.

The Chinese-opera stage was set up outdoors and the audience sat on the ground. Several people, adults as well as kids, had newspaper rolled up into batons that they were selling for one baht a pop—they were for people to spread out on the ground and then sit on.

At the *likay* stage, people were starting to stake out their spots. Mon bought rolled up newspaper and secured a place near the front. Oan and Kampol asked if they could go walk around some more.

"Careful not to get lost and make sure you hold hands the whole time. I'll wait here at the likay theater for you. And don't be gone for too long—the show's about to start. Here's a twenty. If you can't find your way back, ask one of the vendors, okay?"

Oan nodded his head. Hand in hand, the boys made their way back to the merry-go-round, the Ferris wheel, and then over to the train. They debated for a long time before finally jumping on the train for ten baht apiece.

Kampol and Oan beamed as the train prepared to depart. Some parents had come with their kids and were waving; others had climbed on alongside their children. Once the train started moving, the sea of faces glided by, and passengers hollered to people they knew. Where the train drew close to the Ferris wheel, riders on both caught only a quick glimpse of each other, with the Ferris wheel continuing to circle skyward and the train continuing to chug on ahead. The entertainment had started now—as was the shrine's tradition, the Chinese opera was the first to start, and the train riders got a piercing earful of it as they passed one of the theater's huge speakers. When the tracks curved around the stage they were approaching another set of speakers, so the passengers were on guard and ready to plug their ears. As they cruised by the shooting gallery, someone pinged King Kong's target, and the ape shook and growled until the attendant stood the target upright again. After he'd calmed down, the legendary and fearsome ghost Mae Nak began wailing and calling out for her beloved Pi Mak. Other ghostly figures soon joined her with their own menacing sounds, even King Kong roaring once again. Kampol and Oan giggled themselves silly. They could still hear Mae Nak's moaning in the distance long after the train had moved away.

Then an announcement came over the loudspeakers: "Could the parents of Somkid—a six-year-old girl with braids wearing a pink skirt—please come pick her up at the information booth in front of the Chinese-opera theater?" When the train rolled by the booth, Kampol saw the girl sitting on a chair next to the donation box and crying.

"I have an idea! Let's have them page my mama to come and get us," Oan said, thinking it would be funny.

Kampol agreed to play along. After they hopped off the ride, Oan bought a cone of shaved ice with half red syrup, half green, and the whole thing generously drizzled with condensed milk. Kampol chose blue cotton candy, fluffy as a cloud. Then they headed over to the information booth. The announcements quickly followed:

"Prasit Gaewton, or Oan, five years old, has gotten separated from his mother. He's currently at the information kiosk. Could his mother, Mrs. Mon Gaewton, please come pick him up at the information kiosk in front of the Chinese-opera theater?"

"Kampol Changsamran, five years old, is currently at the information kiosk. Could his mother, Mrs. Namfon Changsamran, please come pick him up at the information kiosk in front of the Chinese-opera theater?"

Oan and Kampol sat down next to the girl named Somkid and took turns eating the shaved ice and cotton candy, swapping back and forth. A minute later, Somkid's mother scrambled over, visibly distressed, but she grinned as she hurried toward her daughter with open arms. Meanwhile, Mon had parked herself in front of the likay stage and didn't hear the public announcement, even though it was repeated several times. She realized that she was being paged only when the *ranat* xylophone stopped playing—then, hearing her name, she jumped up. As soon as she rose, someone swooped in to take her spot.

Oan burst out laughing when he saw his mother's face. Figuring out that she'd been pranked, Mon huffed and swore that she'd teach him a lesson. But Kampol refused to get up from his chair.

"Quit playing," Oan told him. "Let's go watch the likay."

"In a minute. You go ahead. In case my mama's here and she hears the PA."

Mon stood for a moment, looking at Kampol. "If your mama doesn't make it, come find me over at the theater, all right?"

Kampol nodded. Slumped in his chair next to the donation box, he swung his legs back and forth as he listened as if hypnotized: "Mrs. Namfon Changsamran... Mrs. Namfon Changsamran, please pick up your son at the information kiosk in front of the Chinese-opera theater."

...Make a Person Want to Eat

On days when he couldn't find any buddies to drink with in the evening, Dum would go around looking for Kampol, yelling and making lots of noise in the process. Dinner at Dum's was usually sticky rice and papaya salad, but the grilled dish varied, sometimes chicken and sometimes pork, and the meat salad switched between *larb* and *nam tok*. Once his whiskey bottle was empty, Dum would inevitably forget that the kid was staying over. At his house, there was only one bed, and once asleep, Dum tossed and turned, throwing his arms around, and he invariably ended up smacking Kampol multiple times. Every time, eventually, Kampol got pushed off the bed and had to drag his pillow down and sleep on the floor below the bed.

Tongbai also had Kampol over for dinner regularly. But each time, before they sat down to eat, Kampol had to help her wash a huge pile of dishes. Even so, they usually weren't able to get done quick enough—when her husband, Gaew, came into the kitchen and saw that there wasn't a plate or bowl he could use for his rice, he complained. Tongbai snapped right back at him. The couple would squabble until the first bites of food made it into their mouths. Only then would they quiet down. After dinner, they never bothered with the dishes; they simply left them to soak. The evening would conclude with them lying down and watching TV until they fell asleep.

Kampol liked staying at Old Jai's. The big, rundown wooden house was livelier than all the other homes. Old Noi's family rented part of the house. They had seven grandchildren between the two of them. Because the house didn't have a television, when night fell, the kids came together and played. They always made a racket but no one tried to force them to keep it down. Whenever Kampol stayed over there, he got to join in on the fun, too. The only problem was the food wasn't very good, regardless of whether it came from Old Noi's or Old Jai's kitchen. Everybody there mostly ate vegetables with a dip of chili paste and nothing else. Kampol hadn't learned to like chili paste, so every time he slept over there, all he had to eat was rice sprinkled with fish sauce, but he still liked staying there regardless.

Kampol stayed at Mon's more often than anywhere else. He kept his clothes there, and Mon was the one who washed them for him. He and Oan had been classmates in first grade, and Oan would always bring him the news from school. The academic year was going to be over in a few days, at which point Oan would be finished with first grade. Listening to his stories, Kampol felt wistful—he really wanted to go back to school. Mon suggested that, since Chong the grocer liked to read, if Kampol was not in school, he should spend as much time as possible with Chong, so that the grocer could tutor him.

She was right: anytime Kampol spent the night at his place, Chong would take out a book and read to him. The shelves in his bedroom were stuffed with books, which then overflowed onto his table and bedside. But the stories Chong read to Kampol often left him confused, even when, afterward, Chong retold them as if they were fables or fairy tales. Still, the stories were sad and often made Kampol cry.

One time, Chong read Kampol a story about a man who hadn't had anything to eat for three days. He went around staring at the food displayed in glass cases at restaurants, all the while feeling faint because he'd put nothing in his stomach for so long. Then he imagined the crunch of a boiled egg being cracked against a steel plate. The memory of the sound reminded him of the taste of a boiled egg. With all the energy he could muster, he went out onto the street and slit a person's throat with a knife, to steal nothing more than the paltry sum of money for a boiled egg. This story haunted Kampol for days. Chong told him over and over again that if he felt hungry or nobody called him at a mealtime, he should come and get himself something at the shop, because extreme hunger could make a person lose control and hurt someone.

Kampol didn't forget his instructions. He couldn't get the man who killed for a boiled egg out of his mind. He studied the people walking up and down the street. When he really looked closely at each one, he realized that almost everybody looked rather hungry. But he wanted to find the person who was starving the most. He set about his task by wandering beyond Mrs. Tongjan's neighborhood and into the old housing development down the street, which was crowded and full of hungry people. But he was searching for the most famished of them all.

Finally, he came upon someone. The man was gaunt and had a withered face; his hair hung matted to the base of his neck; his shirt and pants were filthy. Kampol found him sitting in front of a noodle shop on the side of the main road, mumbling to himself. From the look of him, he might not have eaten for a month. When Kampol spoke to him, he replied in a way that sounded deranged—Kampol couldn't make out what he was talking about. *This is it…this man is terribly hungry*, Kampol thought. *He might lose control and hurt someone.* So, Kampol led the starved man back to Chong's grocery.

"Hia Chong, this man's incredibly hungry," Kampol told him. "He's no longer in control of himself, but he still hasn't hurt anybody yet."

Chong looked at Kampol, utterly stunned for a moment. When he snapped out of it, he hurried into the kitchen to fetch the man something to eat. The man appeared unaware of his surroundings and muttered to himself as Chong handed him the food.

"What about you, Boy? Where are you going to eat this evening? Do you want to eat with me here?" Chong asked.

"I'm eating at Jua's this evening but thank you," Kampol replied.

The starved man carried his plate of food outside and sat down next to the jasmine bush, where he continued ranting something under his breath with his gaze toward the sky. Kampol and Chong, watching, rooted for him to lift the spoon to his mouth.

A New Home

Wasu Changsamran—or Ratom to those who still called him by his old name, which he changed when his youngest son was born—had good news for Kampol the next time he came to visit: they had a new home.

Kampol packed his clothes, excited. He made the rounds to the different homes where he had stayed to say goodbye, running from one to the next. Wasu followed him, thanking the neighbors for showing his son such kindness.

"May the heat and hardship be gone for good," Dum said as a blessing.

"Be sure to go to school next year!" was Mon's parting instruction.

"Hey! Wait!" Jua shouted. "You left some clothes at my house."

"Come back and visit us from time to time," Chong told him.

"Be well, the best of luck. May you find joy and comfort ahead."

"Good luck, good luck."

"Goodbye."

Kampol waved. He kept glancing side to side, at once

happy but also in shock to be leaving his friends. Oan caught up with him, handed him a small action figure, and ran home.

Outside the new house, Wasu's ex-wife—whom Wasu had been married to before Namfon and had now conveniently taken up with again—was hanging cloth diapers on a clothesline. When she turned around and saw Wasu, Kampol, and his bag of clothes, her brow furrowed and her jaw dropped—she looked shocked. But she didn't say a word; she simply spun back around and carried on with shaking out the laundry and placing it on the line—diapers, tiny shorts, miniscule shirts.

Wasu smiled sheepishly. "You're doing laundry, then? Boy, come here. Say hi to Mama Lim."

Kampol brought his palms together and *waied* her very politely. Mama Lim turned and gave him the barest of smiles.

"Come here. I want to show you something." With a tug, Wasu steered his son inside.

There, Jon, Kampol's baby brother, was sitting up in his metal crib. When he saw Kampol and his father, he pulled himself up by grabbing onto the crossbar. Kampol squealed and ran over to hug his little brother. "Papa, look! Jon can stand!"

"Oh yeah…and you haven't seen this. Let me show you."

Wasu lifted Jon out of the crib, stood him on the ground, let go, and backed away. "Come here, you, come to Papa, come, little guy, come!" Jon looked at their father, giggled, and started taking steps: one, two, three, four, five, six. The toddler came within reach of their father before he lost his balance, and Wasu caught him before he tumbled.

"Six steps! Jon made it six steps!" Kampol said, jumping up and down.

The three of them shared a hearty laugh.

Mama Lim spoke very little. She was constantly moving, picking up something or dealing with some task. She earned her living primarily as a laundress. In the house, she had a massive garment rack that was always full of clothes that had been pressed and put on hangers. The whole room Wasu and his sons were in was infused with the pleasant smell of clean laundry. Kampol breathed it in deeply, feeling wonderful. Mama Lim had come inside, but now she finished the ironing and went back out to do some more washing. Kampol was looking after his brother, and their father left to work his shift delivering water on his truck. He would be back around dinnertime.

That evening, Mama Lim made *palo* egg stew. The aroma of it alone had Kampol salivating, but he had to hold back until his father got home so they could all have dinner together. Mama Lim sat out front waiting for Wasu to arrive. Kampol, feeling upbeat, thought it would be fun to hide behind the shoe cabinet so that he could ambush his father with a "Boo!" when he came into the room. It was just before dark when his father returned home.

"Wasu, we need to talk before we go inside," Mama Lim said, intercepting him. "Are you bringing the boy here for a visit or to stay?"

"Let him stay for now, okay? It's just one kid. And seeing that I've already brought him here…"

"I've already got all I can handle with Jon. There's simply no way. And we're about to run out of formula again. Did you get some money? I've already spotted you for several cans."

"Can you spot me again for now?"

"Fine, but after dinner, take Boy back. And do it today— the longer he stays, the harder it'll be on him."

Wasu sighed, his head drooping. As he came inside the

house, Kampol remained crouched down in silence. He forgot to shout "Boo!" at his father.

With everyone home, it was time to dig into dinner. Mama Lim and his father both gave Kampol their eggs.

"What a pity!" Wasu exclaimed. "Mama Lim has to go to the hospital for several days. Boy, you'll have to go back and stay in the old neighborhood for now, okay? After she gets out of the hospital, I'll come get you again, all right, son?"

Before leaving, Kampol went over to the crib. He looked at his baby brother for a long time. Then he grabbed something.

"What did you just take?" Mama Lim immediately asked.

"It's mine." Kampol said, holding out his action figure, and just before his hatred showed in his eyes, his father led him out of the house.

In the dark, father and son walked without talking until they reached the front of Chong's grocery.

Wasu set Kampol's bag down. He leaned in and whispered: "I'm going to have to leave you here. You call for Hia Chong in a second, all right? I'm off. Good luck, son."

Kampol watched his father walk off until he disappeared. The flavor of the palo stew had grown distant, and the scent of detergent faint. He opened his hand: the blue action figure glinted in the dim light.

Pony Express

The grocery had a telephone now. Chong had purchased a big red pay phone and had it installed in the front of his shop. The children were excited by the development and ran to tell their parents. Customers coming into the store to do their shopping tossed glances at the shiny new red telephone. Within a few days, the community members all carried the telephone numbers of their friends and family in their pockets, both immediate and extended. Everyone suddenly had important business that required regular use of a phone. It didn't take long until they were griping about how much money they'd dropped making calls. So, they tried to come up with a new strategy. Some smart cookie went and asked Chong for the shop's phone number. Within a few days, everybody in Mrs. Tongjan's community had the number.

For Chong, it was total chaos. The phone rang off the hook—callers asking to speak with various neighbors. He kept having to leave the shop unattended to go fetch whomever was requested. After a couple of weeks, he began getting aggravated. He appealed to them, asking them diplomatically to please only have people call the phone for truly urgent business. But they told him it couldn't be helped, since they weren't the ones making the calls. Thus, a new policy was put in place: anyone who received a call had to pay a five-baht service fee.

The profits fell right into Kampol's lap. He became the pony express, sprinting off to get people for their calls, and as soon as they hung up, he was right there to demand the service fee. Kampol became so rich he had to buy a piggy bank. Many of the other children watched him making money enviously. Since he didn't have time for it anymore, he relinquished the job of being Dang's masseur to Oan. He also allowed his friend Jua to serve as a limping messenger once or twice a day. Chong was relieved to be able to extricate himself from the task.

The unit that Kampol's family had once lived in was no longer empty. The new tenant was a small man, very neatly dressed. He had wavy hair that he always combed back with oil. He owned a motorcycle, though not a single person knew what his occupation was. One week into living in the community, the man visited the grocery store, and asked for the phone number so that he could be reached for his work, telling Chong only that his name was Bangkerd.

The first time he got a call, when Chong answered the phone, all he heard was sobbing. The caller wept as she spoke: her son had died, and the body was at the hospital. The temple had given her this number for Bangkerd the mortician so she could get him to come prepare the body. Chong told her to hold on.

"Whose call is it, Hia Chong?" Kampol asked, set to run.

"It's all right. I'll go myself."

The mortician came to take the call. He said only a couple of words and then hung up. When he went to pay the service fee, Chong refused it, shaking his head. Kampol was puzzled as he witnessed the interaction.

All the excitement about the phone started to die down, so Kampol's business grew sluggish. But his piggy bank was more than half full of five-baht coins by then, and it weighed a ton. He only got to carry a message every few days. Only Bangkerd the mortician still received calls regularly. But each call to him meant that someone had died. From every which way, news of death funneled through the red telephone and into Chong's consciousness, before he relayed it to Bangkerd. Chong grew more and more somber every time he took one of those calls, even though he continued to be willing to inform the man himself and never charged him.

The whole time Kampol kept wondering. He didn't understand why Chong didn't charge Bangkerd a service fee. One day, he was sitting around just waiting, bored. He hadn't had to go fetch anyone for a call in days, and all his friends had disappeared. Kampol gave up and went off to find his playmates.

In the older housing development down the road, Kampol happened to pass by the home of Tia, the short, cheeky fisherman universally loved by the children. Whenever they ran into him, they formed a line behind him and followed him wherever he went. Tia was a funny guy. He regaled the children with hilarious anecdotes that bordered on the inappropriate, and he never repeated the same story twice. But for some unknown reason, many of the adults, in particular the women, didn't care for him.

Kampol stopped outside Tia's house and looked in. Through the upstairs window, he saw Tia's head bouncing up and down.

"Uncle Tia," Kampol yelled, "have you seen Oan or Jua?"

Tia poked his head out and looked down. He was up to something that Kampol didn't understand. He was panting and bumping up and down as if he were on horseback. He sneered at Kampol then shouted, "I don't fucking know."

Kampol kept watching. It was very curious the way Tia's body was moving, it looked like he was riding the merry-go-round at the shrine fair, except on a faster horse and didn't rotate.

"What are you doing?" Kampol asked, picturing a wooden horse swaying back and forth. "Are you riding a rocking horse?"

Tia flashed his canines. "Oh yeah, I saw Oan over there!" Kampol stared up at the window for a while longer before he left to look for Oan. That evening, after he'd returned to the grocery, the phone rang. Chong answered. Kampol kept his fingers crossed, hoping to get the job.

"What? Tia's dead? How did he die?"

Kampol went numb. He screamed at the top of his lungs, "That's not true, Hia Chong. I just saw Uncle Tia earlier this afternoon—he was riding on a rocking horse."

"What did you say? Where did you see him?"

"At his house. He was on a rocking horse by the window."

Chong looked shaken. "Uncle Tia is dead, Boy. He died riding the horse by the window."

Kampol's face fell and he started crying. He missed Tia already. This time, he went to find Bangkerd himself and turned down the money when the mortician tried to pay him.

The Funeral

Tia's death came like a bolt from the blue. The children all mourned his passing: from now on, there would be nobody to tell them fun tales; around the bends of the river, streams, and swamps, there would no longer be the short man with his fishing gear.

Tia's funeral was planned for a single evening at the Samed Temple. His daughter, who had her own family and lived in another province, had come back to organize her father's rites upon receiving the news. The photo next to the casket was from his national ID card, complete with the height ruler in the background—he had only been one hundred and forty-five centimeters tall. His face looked dark and scary in the picture. He had been exactly sixty years old.

Kampol and his friends joined up, over ten of them in all, to head to Tia's funeral together. The temple was just under two kilometers away. Several of the kids went to the Samed Temple School so they were used to the walk. Kampol, Oan, and the lame-legged Jua, because they were smaller than the others, had a harder time. They needed to walk a bit then run a bit to keep up with the bigger kids. The three of them were afraid of the dark.

At the pavilion where the body was, five adults were running around, and three cooks, in the kitchen behind, were making fish-and-rice porridge. A group of more than ten kids from the older housing development had also shown up for the funeral. They were hanging out by the steps of the crematorium. Kampol's crew marched straight to a guest table when they arrived and sat down. The kids from the other development snickered. One of the grown-ups came out and shooed them away with the wave of a hand. Awkward and embarrassed, Kampol and his friends got up, revealing their feet that were covered in dirt from the walk. They stood around clumsily trying to stay out of the way by moving over to one side. Eventually, they claimed the steps that led up to the kitchen.

"Hey! I smell fish porridge!" somebody in the group exclaimed.

"You think they'll let us have some?"

"Of course. We're here for the funeral."

"You dumbass. You've got to give them an envelope with money, otherwise they don't feed you. They only let people with envelopes sit at the tables."

"You're back again?" one of the cooks snapped, standing over them. "I just told you to get lost, and here you are again running your loud mouths. Get out of here! Don't you have some place to go and play?"

Because they didn't know where to go, they went over and sat with the kids from the other development on the steps of the crematorium.

The monks were already chanting, but no guests had arrived. The tables and chairs set up in front of the pavilion were completely empty. The kids got spooked by the whistling wind. Kampol told everyone about how he'd seen Tia through the window before the fisherman died. Everyone's hair stood on end thinking about how they'd have to walk by the dead man's house later. The kids from the other development, ready to take off, nudged each other. Kampol and his group kept looking at one another, before finally deciding to follow after the other bunch.

The kids, about twenty-five of them all together, walked in a pack, kicking up a haze of dust as they went. They made a lot of noise and played pranks on one another until some of the smaller kids broke into tears. Tia's funeral had come and gone for them, though they could still hear the monks' humming prayers channeled to them by the wind.

Meanwhile, Tia's daughter was complaining to the cooks. She didn't understand why no one had shown up for her father's funeral.

"Don't take this as me speaking ill of the dead, but it's kind of common knowledge that he was a lech," a cook told her.

"Yeah, he liked to move in on other people's wives," the second cook added.

"One time, he took Song's wife out into the fields and they had sex. When Song found out, he brought a bunch of his friends and they beat Tia silly. But he still didn't learn his lesson. When he healed, he was chasing her again," the third cook shared.

"Some women were really into him. They went behind their husbands' backs to meet up with him."

"The young women sure didn't like him, though. They've all been on the receiving end of his raunchiness at least once or twice. By the end, everybody avoided even passing him on the street."

"Yeah, most of the men were mad at him and the women didn't dare show up because they were afraid their husbands would suspect they had something going on with Tia. And the young women…you can forget about them. That's why no one's here."

"But strangely, the kids really loved him. I don't know how he did it, but he always had them in stitches."

"Yeah, he gave them fish, sometimes, too."

"So maybe *that's* why. And what the mortician said—how Papa died having sex—is that true?"

The second cook looked horrified and turned red. The other two eyed her suspiciously.

The cremation took place a few days later. Oan was at school, but Kampol and Jua showed up and waited, hoping to snatch some money in the alms toss. But even before the Samed Temple School let out for the day, the students were already mobbing the front of the crematorium. Jua ended up having to stand back and watch because he was worried about getting trampled. Kampol came out of the stampede with a black eye and not a single coin.

Pretty soon, the students scattered toward home. As they walked away, they peeled the yellow cellophane off the coins, pocketing the money and dumping the wrappers in their wake. On their walk back to the housing development, Kampol and Jua made a competition of collecting the discarded cellophane.

The two of them smoothed out the wrappers and popped them over their eyes, giggling the whole time. They had transformed the world into yellow gold.

The Pine Trees

To exit onto the main road from Mrs. Tongjan's housing development, you had to pass the Cheunjit Bungalows. The side of the vacation property bordering the street was protected by a brick wall taller than head-high. On the other side, the back fence was bricks only on the lower half; the top part was barbed wire. Along the inside of the fence stood ten enormous pine trees, all in a row, forming a fortress. Their tapered tops poked high into the sky. Even from far down the main road, they could be easily spotted. Chong admired those towering pines very much. He said they were ancient, well formed, and elegant—the tallest he'd ever seen.

One night, Kampol fell asleep at Mon's house, and finding his mother standing over him when he woke up felt like a dream.

"Boy, get up quick. Come and sleep with Mama."

Kampol was astonished, but he didn't rush into her arms. He simply stared at her, confused. He had stopped expecting her to return.

His mom, with tears running down her face, took Kampol in her arms and carried him out of the house.

Kampol had his arms wrapped around her neck and his head resting on her shoulder. As they made their way in the dark, he could hear her sniffing. He wanted to know where they were going: Was she taking him to come live with her in her new home?

Before long, they reached their destination. Namfon turned into the entrance to the Cheunjit Bungalows. Kampol was awed. He had lived in the neighborhood his whole life, but this was the first time he'd ever entered the part of the property with the bungalows.

"We'll spend the night here, sweetie."

The bungalows were like little houses, and there were many of them, each with its own front porch and a parking space along the side. Kampol took in the sight, but his eyes soon started swimming and he couldn't keep straight which bungalow was which: they all looked identical to him. His mother used a key to unlock one of the units. Inside was a bed and a small table, and that was it.

"Do you live here?" Kampol asked.

His mother laughed but didn't answer him. Instead, she asked Kampol to tell her about his father and brother. Mother and son fell asleep chatting.

Kampol wasn't awake for any of it, but at one in the morning someone knocked on the door. His mother carried him, draped over her shoulder, back to Mon's. In the morning, he woke up with Oan lying next to him. Startled, he began to doubt himself: Had his mother really come to see him or had it just been a dream?

In a daze, Kampol walked over to the bungalows. Oan came along, too. The security guard out front knew the two of them well but wasn't going to allow them to enter.

"My mother's in there. Last night I spent the night in there with her."

The guard shook his head and shooed the kids out of

the way. He bowed to a car exiting the property.

Kampol refused to give up. He went around to the back fence and shoved his way through the mess of reeds that ran along it. Oan held the barbed wire open for him, and Kampol slipped in. He turned to do the same for his friend, but Oan had frozen up: an old man with a rake leaned against one of the pine trees. Smoking a cigarette, he eyed the intruders as if gazing at morning clouds.

"What's up, guys? What business brings you here?"

"That's Sae's grandpa, Sae from the old housing development…" Oan whispered to Kampol.

"I'm looking for my mama. She's in here," Kampol told the man, his voice trembling.

"Namfon, right? She's left already," Sae's grandfather told them. He took another puff and pointed. "Over there, in that unit. Your mama often stays there."

Every single day from then on, Kampol walked along the back fence, and he eventually trampled the tall jungle grass along it flat. A bunch of the other kids came along. For them, it was somewhere new, and it was pleasantly shady under the pines. When Sae's grandpa raked up the fallen needles, he chucked them over the fence, so the children laid down on a carpet of pine foliage and rolled around contentedly.

Kampol kept an eye out for his mother. His friends helped, too, all of them eagerly monitoring each car that passed. They came back in the evenings, even after they'd showered and eaten dinner, to resume looking out. The corpulent manager of the bungalows once came to issue a threat: if their noise disturbed his guests, he would hand them over to the police.

One night, there was drama: A woman burst out of a car, screaming. She fled to the back of the property. Kampol and his crew watched her in utter shock. She tried to squeeze through the fence, but the barbed wire snagged her shirt. Noi rushed to free her.

"Help me, kids! Help me!" she cried.

The children zealously came to her aid. When they got her free, they ran with her into the night, making sure to avoid any lights until they reached the grocery store. Chong was visibly amazed. Once he'd pieced the story together, he took the woman and the children upstairs to hide. Soon thereafter a car drove through the neighborhood, slowing down as it approached the store. Chong sat there watching TV, his heart about to jump out of his chest. The car circled in front of the rows of houses and then drove off. Chong then let the children go home one at a time, except for Kampol. As for the young woman, she waited until four in the morning to leave.

The story made the rounds of the whole neighborhood, and the fat bungalow manager was angry. The events prompted him to call workmen to come and take down the barbed wire from the back fence and build a high wall like the one on the street side instead. And he took an even more drastic measure: he eliminated the expense of employing a landscaper by having the workmen cut down the pine trees at the same time.

In the older housing development, Sae's grandpa fell ill. After twenty years of working every day as a landscaper, he was idle for the first time.

Chong was mournful as he watched the tree-cutting operation. The workers sawed off one section at a time, starting from the crown and working their way down. The pines disappeared, one top at a time, one tree at a time.

Kampol stood next to Chong, staring upward until the sky was empty. The notion of his mother, too, grew empty in his mind.

The Flea Markets

Along the main road, near the exit from Mrs. Tongjan's housing development, were two large businesses right across from
one another. On the right was TrueWare, which sold all kinds
of hardware. On the left was Modium, which sold home dé-
cor products. The two weren't competitors, but they'd fallen
into the same predicament: they were struggling and on their
last legs. TrueWare was the first to make a move.

A giant sign went up, announcing TrueWare would host
a flea market in their parking lot each Friday, Saturday, and
Sunday evening. Interested sellers could contact them to re-
serve a spot. It worked. People went crazy over it and flocked
to the place. The lot was crammed with goods and shoppers.
The children from Mrs. Tongjan's neighborhood were excited
by the new development. They walked all over the market until they got tired; they had no money to buy anything, so they
decided they wanted to become vendors, instead.

Kampol convinced Chong to give him ten cassettes and
ten used books. Jua's mother lugged home some old books
from the paper-baling plant—there were comics, books about
the dharma, and cookbooks in the mix. Because it happened
to be a school vacation, everyone's parents were supportive

and helped dig up old things that still might be usable for their children to sell. Some of them foraged for water spinach and made bundles for their kids. Oan and Noi's parents didn't have any old stuff lying around, so they partnered up and went to pick Manila tamarinds from the trees that grew in some giant reeds. On their way back, they got stung by hornets, once each—Noi on his upper left eyelid and Oan on his lower right. Soon they looked like twins with their misshapen eyes on opposite sides.

The kids set up a straw mat where there was a vacant space just inside the market's gate. They got evicted within ten minutes. A woman informed them that she had reserved the spot, and had already paid for it. The children stood up, rolled up the mat, and each of them scrambled to collect his merchandise. They moved to another spot that was still unoccupied. But before they even sat down, the rightful renter showed up again. No matter where they tried to set up shop, there wasn't a single space that hadn't been reserved. The children began to lose heart.

"Hey, you rascals have to go over there. Past that post there," a doll seller said, pointing helpfully.

The kids unrolled their straw mat and arranged their wares once more, looking out for anyone who might be coming to boot them out. While they watched in front of them, a bald man wearing a ridiculously short necktie was coming straight for them from behind, and he looked mad. He told them they would have to pay rent, but they didn't have the money. So, the mat was rolled up once again.

Since they weren't allowed to set up inside, the children decided to lay out their mat just beyond the property, out by the road. And even though their spot was unlit, it seemed as if they'd snagged themselves the best location of all.

A week later, Modium followed suit and offered up their parking lot for reservations as well. Their flea market would take place every Thursday, Friday, Saturday, and Sunday evening. With their rent being cheaper than TrueWare's, the vendors all moved over to Modium. The customers followed, and now it was Modium's parking lot that they all crammed into. The children's operation moved with the crowd. As before, they claimed an area by the road just outside the gate.

The bald manager of TrueWare came up with a new strategy in a hurry, announcing that the rent would be cut in half. But only about half of the vendors came back. The manager weighed his options, scratching his hairless head. The next day he went to check out the market outside of Modium, and he noticed a throng of people clustered around one spot. The point of interest was none other than the children's stall.

"What are you cuties selling today?" a woman cooed, obviously finding the children endearing.

"Can I see that dharma book?"

"These school uniform shoes are only twenty baht?"

"I'll take a bag of those Manila tamarinds. Did the hornets get you again?"

Of course! The shoppers had fallen for the adorable little kids. The bald manager's eyes shined. The next day, he went on a mission to track down the children. He asked all over the place, eventually ending up at Mrs. Tongjan's housing project.

"From now on, you can come right in to sell your things," the bald manager told them. "I'll arrange a prime location for you, and you don't have to pay a single baht in rent."

The children listened, their faces expressionless. They weren't interested. They were doing even brisker business outside the market than in. The manager flicked abacus beads in his head.

"All right, you can set up outside, but if you do it in front of TrueWare instead of Modium, I'll give you twenty baht each."

The children's faces lit up. They accepted his offer, sealing the deal with nodding heads.

Week after week, TrueWare and Modium invented new schemes to edge out the other, neither of them willing to back down. But daily and nightly the world of business keeps spinning. One shrewd investor had been watching the two companies duel it out. He owned an empty plot of land a mere five hundred meters down the road. Within two months, he unveiled his own grand project.

Chatuchak Market, named after the mother of all flea markets in Bangkok, started leasing spaces both short or long term, all kinds of goods welcome. It offered conveniences like bathrooms and a sprawling parking lot. TrueWare and Modium, having fought each other till their last breaths, finally threw in the towel, surrendering to the world of business.

But the children were left scratching their heads. There was no more TrueWare Market or Modium Market, both of which had become almost a part of the neighborhood. Now there was only Chatuchak Market, with all its unfamiliar faces. Finally, they figured they might as well share the comic books amongst themselves, divvying up the Manila tamarinds.

Lucky Kid

One Saturday evening, as the sun was softening, playtime was drawing to a close, but the shrieks and shouts of the kids weren't letting up at all.

Mrs. Tongjan had a little dog, Momo, who was growing out of being a little puppy. At five months old, he was growing rambunctious and wanted to chew everything he could get his mouth on. Mrs. Tongjan's doormat got chewed to shreds. Her laundry brush got maimed by his sharp fangs. The clothes she had hanging on the line got yanked down and dragged through the dirt. Momo would bite down on them and then shake his head wildly. Mrs. Tongjan's son's pants had been turned into rags. That evening, Momo was running circles around the house like a hunting dog chasing some poor rabbit. But then he paused, and his ears perked up as he listened to something.

Eyes glaring, ears pricked, and hair bristled on his back, Momo trotted toward his victim.

The unfortunate child was Ploy, Penporn's older sister. One or two of the kids witnessed the moment Momo bit Ploy. The game they had been playing came to an immediate halt when yelps of pain exploded. But quickly, movement resumed. The kids, in total chaos, scurried off to tell their parents about the incident. Kampol went to tell Chong.

"Mo bit Ploy on the butt."

Puang, Ploy's mother, ran over, panicked, with lots of other people following behind her. Jua remarked to everyone, "Looks like Momo's gone mad."

The poor girl, Ploy, just now being held on someone's lap, was handed over to her mother. Puang pulled her daughter's pants down to inspect the wound. There were deep fang marks, four of them. All around the girl and her mother, people watched with looks of horror on their faces, but Puang was more scared than anyone. She held her daughter close, trying to calm her down, but she was sniveling herself. When Puang figured out that the culprit dog was Mrs. Tongjan's, she screamed and cursed, relinquishing all common decency.

Momo was locked up inside the house. Mrs. Tongjan's son backed his car out of the garage.

"All right, save the blame for later. Get the kid in the car and let's go to the doctor first." Mrs. Tongjan came out to oversee the situation as well.

The car drove off as everyone watched. Mrs. Tongjan was in the passenger seat, next to her son, who was driving. Puang was in the back, with Ploy lying prone over her lap. Ampan, Ploy's older sister, went with them, too.

The following day, Momo was still confined to the house. The children, gun-shy, were afraid to come out and play. They sat, stunned, remembering how things had once been, when Momo had first arrived, and he'd been a tiny puppy. He used to run after the neighborhood children and roll around in the mud and sand with every single one of them. How could he have disregarded those past friendships and turn around and bite an old pal?

Kampol and Jua were mopily sitting by the patient's bedside. So many friends of Ploy's had been popping in and out that Old Noi's house was dotted with dirty footprints. The grown-ups each paid a visit as well, taking turns to stop by. Chong brought a six pack of small cartons of milk and several other snacks. The children's eyes lit up when they saw the gifts.

And then Mrs. Tongjan made an appearance. Everyone made way for her and the glorious, gigantic care basket in her hands. Fresh fruit, canned fruit, bread, condensed milk, and fine treats—expensive ones that the children had never even seen in Chong's store—were arranged in the basket, which was covered with plastic wrap and decorated with red ribbons tied into a big bow. It was magnificent.

Ploy's friends had to gulp down their saliva. Some of their mouths were gaped open, and all eyes were glued to the array of gifts. The patient herself was lying on her stomach with her face turned toward the basket, cheeks flushed. With her half smile, she looked incredibly happy.

In the evening, Kampol and Jua wandered toward Mrs. Tongjan's house. The two were sketching out dreams in their heads, but neither of them said a word to the other. Eventually, they plunked themselves down by a sandpit. It was here that Momo the puppy had liked to dig when he played with them.

Kampol was imagining: How would it be if he, too, got bitten by the dog? But suddenly he jumped—because Jua had shouted.

"Stupid Mo! You should have bitten me!" And then, with all his might, Jua hurled the sand he'd been holding tight in his fist.

Kampol followed suit, flinging a fistful of sand toward Mrs. Tongjan's house.

"Come and get me, Mo!"

The Rice Giveaway

Mon locked up. Her three-person household—mother, father, and son—were going, with one more person in tow: Kampol. Tongbai was going with her husband, Gaew. Noi was going with his mother and sister. Old Jai's entire family was going: his daughter, son, son-in-law, daughter-in-law, plus four grandchildren. Old Noi was staying behind to watch the house. Puang was going with her husband and all three of her daughters. Od, Rah, and Chai were going together as a group.

They were all going to the rice giveaway at the Zeng Tek Xiang Tung Shrine. Not a single person who didn't have to work was missing the opportunity. Children, big and small, pulled equal weight: one life equaled one bag of rice. Even infants who couldn't crawl yet were accorded the same status. Pregnant women received two bags, one for the baby in their belly.

The crowd was massive, but only half of the people were locals. The rest had traveled from elsewhere, some from as far away as another district or even another province. Large trucks, many, many of them, had brought people for the free rice. The people they brought knew better than the locals where and when the rice giveaways would take place. It was how they made their living.

Before noon, an announcement came, telling everyone to come and wait inside the shrine's gate. The vendors outside were doing such brisk business that their hands were like wheels spinning yarn. Everybody bought drinks and, for lunch, something small to tide them over.

Inside the gate, spaces under trees or any kind of shade were hard to come by. Most people were left searing in the sun. The men and the young people, unperturbed by the heat, gravitated toward the exit, positioning themselves to be among the first to receive free rice. The pregnant women, grannies, and mothers who had brought babies with them were the ones to sacrifice: they stood back and let the others go ahead of them. But once the whole crowd had come inside and was shut in, there was no free space; even shifting a little was a challenge. The sun was scorching, and everybody was dripping sweat, breathing in everyone else's odor, and revealing their own.

People were just about at their limit with getting simmered, and they were ready to shoot out like water bursting through the gates of a dam—they only needed their cue. The staff conducting the giveaway were stationed at the exit now. The truck loaded with white rice was waiting with its tailgate down. With everything in place, the order was given to open the gate.

Now that the crowd had a way to escape, nothing could hold them back. The staff worked efficiently; the rice was swiftly passed out. Hands that got a bag got smeared with red paint, the stain designed to prevent people from coming back for another round.

Kampol moved with the bodies in front of him, and Mon kept a tight grip on his hand. Oan was on his father's back. In the middle of being jostled and squashed along with everybody else, Kampol saw a slice of his mother's face for a second—she was just over there. He got very excited. He yelled for her. In his excitement, his hand unlatched from Mon's. Kampol tried to push forward in hopes of catching up to his mother but it got him nowhere. He shouted and shouted—no reply. He didn't see Mon when he looked back either, and he was being squeezed ever more from all directions. People stepped on his flip-flops and they slipped off his feet, both of them. He couldn't move his body, and his toes were no longer touching the ground. It felt to him like he was stepping on other people's feet the whole time now. Even though he couldn't walk or shift his body, he was moving forward, swept along at the whim of the sea of bodies.

When he looked behind him another time, he saw his father's head, and Jon was wrapped around his neck. Kampol yelled to them. He attempted to crawl higher but his efforts failed, so he just kept shouting. And at last, a reply came through: "Boy, it's Papa, over here. Meet me outside." Kampol was heartened, and because of that, he cried out to each of his parents to relay the news:

"Papa, Mama's just ahead!"

"Mama, Papa's just behind me!"

"Meet me outside, Papa!"

"Meet me outside, Mama!"

"Jon, can you hear me?"

"Mama, Jon's here, too! Meet us outside!"

Kampol was given a bag of rice, and the entire back of one of his hands was smudged with red. He hurried off in search of his mother, who had exited first. The area outside was still teeming with people because everyone was waiting for their family or the folks they'd come with to come out or was wandering around looking for them. Kampol searched and searched until he was worn out. Unable to find his mother, he went back to the mouth of the gate to wait for his father. A little while later, someone tugged at his arm. He turned. It was Oan.

"Here you are. Hurry, people are about to head back home now."

"You go. I told my papa I'd wait for him," Kampol said.

Toward the end, the pregnant ladies, elderly women, and mothers with babies in tow were the only people still passing through the gate. Kampol, wilting in the sun as he sat next to his bag of rice, kept watching until every last person came through. After everyone was out, the gate was slid all the way open. Kampol ran inside to do another sweep. All he found were his flip-flops, lying tossed in different places. By the time he came back outside, the crowd had thinned. He combed the whole area again: neither of his parents were anywhere to be found.

The street was empty. Everybody else had gone home. Kampol lifted the bag of rice onto his right shoulder. When it got tired, he switched the weight over to his left, and then back to the right, and then back to the left. The load was too much for him. He thought about abandoning the rice and was about to when he looked up and saw Chong.

Drained in every way, as soon as Chong put him on his back, he slumped over, asleep.

Dear Moon

A huge moon hung over the roof of Chong's store. And just like that, a familiar place was transformed—the trees, the packed dirt, the street, the utility poles, the roofs of the tenement houses—they were the same yet altered by the spell of the moonlight.

"It's full! It's full!" the kids cheered.

"There! Above Hia Chong's grocery!"

Together the children carried the daybed from beneath the poinciana and set it down under the open sky. Ampan, the oldest of Puang's daughters, and her two friends Bow and Gib, were beginning to stand up straighter and starting to make dreamy eyes when they talked about boys. The three girls, all twelve, had recently finished sixth grade.

The pearly light of the moon sent the three of them into a reverie. They sat on the daybed, carrying on in adolescent whispers. The boys were in a gunfight, riding on horseback. As they waged battle, they admired the sharpness of their own brave shadows on the ground. As for Penporn, she stood quietly, her eyes tracking a soufflé of white clouds, which drifted toward the moon.

Over at Old Noi and Jai's house, all was hushed. The

only children inside were the twins, Gae and Gay, Jai's grand-daughters, who were folding laundry.

"Where are all those rascals?" Noi grumbled. "Gae, Gay, once you're done folding, go and have a look, will you? It's dark out. It's time they come home. That silly Pen's run off with the rest of them, too."

The twins, once they'd headed out, were as lost as the others. Old Noi grabbed her trusty cane and went out after them. She could hear noises coming from the dirt yard in front of the tenements.

"It's so late—don't they know when to quit?" the old lady muttered as she made her way toward the noise. But then she noticed that her path was unusually illuminated. She looked at the sky. "Ah…it's already the full moon again."

Leaning on her cane, Old Noi made it to the daybed. "Here's where you've all been hiding. It's late—aren't you afraid snakes are going to get you?"

"Grandma, look. The moon's hiding behind the clouds again."

Old Noi sat down. For a minute, she got lost gazing at the moon. Then she chuckled. "When I see the full moon, it makes me think of back when I was girl. What fun we had then. Us kids used to sneak out all the time. Oh damn, I'm craving betel nut. Can someone run and get it for me?"

As the old lady pounded her betel-nut mixture, she told of bygone days. "Once, I was really mad at Soon's son, so I ran off to sleep in the barn in the middle of the rice fields. That night happened to be a full moon. He came after me, begging for forgiveness. He brought me palm juice."

"Who was Soon's son, Grandma?"

"It's Keng—your grandpa, silly."

"Oh! We were wondering!" The children laughed.

Old Noi broke off a bit of the mashed betel nut, popped it into her mouth, and started chomping. "All right, all right. Time to go. It's late." But the old lady only managed to get Penporn to come back with her. The rest of them were too stubborn and refused to go home: the three older girls, absorbed in their dreaming, weren't about to get up and leave; the boys were caught up in their hijinks and continued to chase each other around wildly. But their game had changed: now they were attacking each other's shadows. Kampol fired an imaginary round at Oan's, which was twisting like a snake on the ground. But he had to protect his own at the same time because Jua was trying to stomp on its head.

Chong was dragging his metal gate closed. After he had turned off the lights and locked up the store, he stood peering up at the moon.

"Hia Chong, come look from over here," the children hollered.

"What do you say, ladies? Isn't the moon a beauty tonight?"

Gae, one of the twins, giggled. "Hey, Hia Chong, let me tell you something. Those three girls all have crushes on you."

Her twin, Gay, backed her up: "Yeah, they were saying they want to be your girlfriend when they grow up."

"Really? Can you sing? You've got to be able to sing to go out with me."

"Look who's talking! Gae, Gay, you two were saying he was cute, too," Ampan said.

"Hey now, there's no need to fight over me," Chong said, laughing. "Who can sing 'Dear Moon'? Whoever can sing it will win my heart!"

All of them knew the lullaby and belted it out. The boys quit playing and came over to join in:

Moon, O dear Moon,
give us rice and give us curry,
give the baby a ring to wear,
give him a chair so he can sit,
give him a bed if you see fit.

Moon, O dear Moon,
Give him a play to watch of course,
give him a horse or pachyderm,
and if he squirms, give him Granny Choo,
and please give me Grandma Kerd too.

"What about you all? What would you want from the moon?" Chong asked them.

"Money," Jua told him.

"Or even better, money and a bank," Oan said.

"Boy, what about you?"

Kampol considered the question for a moment and then said, "I'd ask for a Grandma Kerd."

Everyone fell quiet, but then Jua broke the silence, "You can't get a Grandma Kerd, the closest you can have is Kerd the mortician. You want that?"

"Stupid Jua, die!" Kampol said, launching himself at Jua's shadow, aiming straight for his chest.

War and Peace

Noi had declared war on his family, but he had retreated and was sitting in silent protest under the poinciana tree. A few minutes ago, just outside his house, his stepfather had stood with his teeth gritted, pointing his finger in Noi's face. Kan, Noi's mother, had stood behind his stepfather, adjusting her sarong over her chest. Then she had shaken her head wearily and gone back inside.

"Don't show your fucking face back here again. I can't even ask you to do one little damn thing," his stepfather shouted before disappearing into the house. He reemerged a minute later carrying Noi's clothes, which he stuffed in the trashcan by the roadside before going back inside again. The fight had been set off by his stepfather telling Noi to go to the store and buy him whiskey and cigarettes. Noi had refused.

Kampol and Oan happened to be hanging out nearby. They'd witnessed the entire sequence of events, and curiously watched to see if Noi would go and retrieve his clothes from the trash. Noi didn't budge an inch. He simply sat, letting fury spew from his eyes.

At noon, his sister, Gib, came home to eat lunch. Since school was on break, she'd taken a babysitting job in the old housing development. Noi glared in her direction as she went inside their house. She reappeared, looking sour, as she headed toward the grocery.

"Gib, come here," Noi called out to his big sister. "What are you going to buy?"

"What else? Cigarettes and whiskey," Gib told him.

"With whose money?"

"Mine—of course."

"Don't buy them. Why are you going to buy them for that asshole?" Noi raised his voice. "He dumped my clothes in the trash. Just wait until he's sleeping, I'm going to sneak in there and smash his head, that bloodsucking leech. He eats here every day, but when has he ever bought food? A fucking loser if I ever saw one—he leeches off of her like a pimp off a prostitute."

"What about your house? He's the one who pays the rent."

"Hah! He rents it so that he can come here and sleep with Mama... And putting out's not enough either, she's got to spend her own money feeding him, too. He treats Mama like a whore..."

Noi got a head-turning slap for that. Still, he didn't relent and kept repeating: "Mama's a whore," over and over. His sister ran away bawling. Noi was alone again, sitting silently under the tree.

Oan, who'd always looked up to Noi and wanted to get in his good graces, sidled up to him and said, "Noi, aren't you going to go dig out your clothes?"

Kampol was right there with him: "Do you want me to go pull them out for you?"

"Don't!" Noi barked.

"Your stepdad's a pimp?" Oan asked, not backing off.

Kampol said, "Your mama whores for him?" This time, Noi's lid blew off.

He snapped his head toward Kampol. "Who the fuck are you to say that? You're going to disrespect my mama?"

Kampol was petrified and his eyes went wide. "No… just…but you said yourself just now…"

"It's my prerogative if I want to say it, but not you, shithead." The words were barely out of his mouth before Noi punched Kampol in the ear.

Kampol stumbled back. His lips pouted as if he were about to break into tears, but he held them in and lunged at Noi even though Noi was far bigger. They grappled, both ending up on the ground, covered in dirt. Kampol didn't hurt Noi at all, and even worse, he got punched a bunch of times more. But a long *riiiiip* brought everything to a screeching halt. Noi's shirt was so old and the fabric worn so thin—with a single yank the whole back came off in Kampol's hand. Kampol took advantage of the opportunity while Noi looked, stupefied, at his scrap of shirt to make a run for it. Oan bolted after him.

Exhausted, Noi sat down hard. He held the torn-off piece of his shirt in his hands. No one knew if he was crying, because no one else dared to approach the poinciana.

At four that afternoon, Kan's front door opened. Noi's stepfather, in his khaki security-guard uniform and with hair neatly combed, walked out and got on the bike leaned against the front of the house. Kan had followed him out and handed him his dinner box in a bag. As he cycled past the poinciana, he turned and smirked at his stepson before riding on, whistling a melody, evidently in a good mood.

"Noi," Kan called to him. "Go get your clothes out of the trash and wash them."

Noi heard her but simply sat there, knowing full well that if he didn't fish his clothes out today, the garbage truck would come by tonight and there'd be nothing left. All the clothes he owned were in that trashcan. Still, he refused to get up, even as evening set in. At times, there was a breeze, and he'd feel a chill down his back.

Kampol, sporting a fat lip and a black eye, was lazing around at Mon's house, where he'd been hiding out since the fight. It was dark now, but he still didn't dare to venture out. When Mon tried to get the story out of him, he wouldn't speak, so it was Oan who told her the whole thing.

Mon left, but returned soon thereafter. She threw the pile of clothes in her arms into a plastic washtub and said: "Wash all of it, both of you together. And don't you dare do a half-assed job."

Oan scooped the water, and Kampol frothed up the detergent. Three shirts and two pairs of pants went into the suds.

"Hey, look. The butt of his pants is ripped," Oan said, poking his finger through the hole.

The two giggled as they washed Noi's clothes. Four hands in unison, scrunching and scrubbing, scrunching and scrubbing.

The Expired Pills

The following school year, Kampol got to reenroll at Baan Huaykapi School, which was where he went to first grade before he dropped out. His father gave Mon one thousand baht to cover his back-to-school expenses. Kampol bought two new school uniforms, a pair of shoes, and two pairs of socks. He still had his old backpack. Tuition was free since it was a public school. His books were also free, all he had to buy were notebooks and pencils.

"How was the first day of school?" Chong asked him. The grocer had already closed up for the day, so he put their dinners on plates and brought them upstairs so the two of them could eat on the balcony. They were having *gunchiang* fried rice.

Kampol rested his plate on his lap. He picked out the slices of sweet Chinese sausage and arranged them in a circle, like red flower petals, along the rim of his plate. Because they were his favorite, he was saving them for last.

"I have to repeat first grade. My friends have all moved on to second," he told Chong.

"It doesn't matter. It might even be a good thing. It means this year you'll know more than everyone else in your class."

"Not everyone. Chukiat and Saowarot flunked and have to stay back, too. Not Oan, though, he passed and is on to second grade this year."

"How old are you now?"

"Six."

"Time flies, doesn't it? I blinked and suddenly you're six. You know, I've known you since you were born."

"Really? So you remember the thing about the contraceptive pills?"

"Huh? What contraceptive pills?" Chong lifted his chin and looked at Kampol.

Kampol chewed in slow motion, his eyes dreamy as he recalled the details of the story he was telling:

"Gae and Gay, Jua's sisters, told us that the reason me, Oan, and Jua are all exactly the same age is because my mother, Oan's mother, and Jua's mother got pregnant at the same time. They had all taken the same expired contraceptives. Jua's mother had gotten them from her factory. They handed them out for free, so she took some for my mother and Oan's mother, too. And then all three of them got pregnant." Kampol stopped talking but continued to think over the story in his mind.

Chong would have burst out laughing had he not been doing his best not to—he was tensing his face to the point that it was twitching, and managed to keep his tight-lipped smile steady. He had had to look away for a good long time, though.

"Did you know about it?" Kampol asked in a whimper, which made Chong pull himself together.

"No...I'd never heard anything about it," Chong said. "Do you know what contraceptive pills actually are?"

"Yeah," Kampol said adamantly. "If a woman doesn't

want to have a baby she takes contraceptive pills to keep it from happening."

Chong nodded. "Right, right—what you've been told is correct."

Kampol's face crumpled, and teardrops fell on his dinner plate. He didn't have a lot of fried rice left, but not a single piece of the gunchiang edging his plate had been touched.

An alarm went off in Chong's head. It had suddenly dawned on him what the boy thought the story meant, so he lifted Kampol onto his lap and tried to console him.

"Why are you crying, huh? I think you're misunderstanding it."

Kampol half spoke, half sniveled, but Chong was able to glean the sense: "There was no need to resort to the pill. It's not like I wanted to be born."

"Oh, Boy, you've got it wrong. You've got it all wrong." But the grocer couldn't come up with a good way to explain it. "It's not like that, all right? It's not like that at all." He dragged out a long sigh, buying himself some time. "Trust me, all right? It's not like that. I was there. I went to the hospital to visit you right after you were born. Your parents were both over the moon. And do you remember when you first started kindergarten, your mother going with you and sticking around until you got out? She even did it the second day, and the third."

Kampol stopped sniffling. Chong's words had transported his mind somewhere else.

"Today, Hia Chong, a bunch of the new kindergartners' parents came and hung around the whole time, too. There was this kid named Piag. His grandma was one of the ones that stayed, and you could hear her calling him, 'Granny's Piag, Granny's Piag.' And she pounded her betel nut right there,

just outside the classroom, and kept spitting out the juice—
ptui, ptui—into a potted plant."

Kampol, laughing at his own story, had Chong chuckling as well.

"My mother stayed with me on my first day, too?…"

Chong was about to say more, but realized that he should stop. Instead, he exclaimed, "Oh! Why aren't you eating your gunchiang? Don't you like it?"

"I do…I was saving them for last."

And then Kampol dug into his gunchiang flower, savoring it a single petal at a time.

A Detective Story: Kids' Edition

"The story goes that once upon a time, there were two friends, Juk and Klae. Juk had a top knot and Klae had pigtails. They were temple wards, and their duty was to carry lunchboxes as they followed the monk on his rounds for alms. One morning, the two found ten baht lying along the side of their route. Juk was quicker to pick up the money, but Klae claimed that he had seen it first, so the money ought to be his. Juk protested and they got into an argument. The Venerable Elder turned around and told them to stop fighting—they could settle the matter back at the temple.

"Once they'd returned, Juk immediately put the lunchbox down and ran off. He went into the banana grove and looked for a good place to hide the money. He dug a hole and buried the ten baht. Fearing that Klae might figure out where he'd hidden the money, he pondered what to do. Then he bent down and wrote in the dirt covering the hole: 'No money is hidden in this hole.'

"Klae watched Juk as he came out of the banana grove, though he pretended to be minding his own business. Then when Juk had gone, he ran into the grove. He hunted around for a while before eventually spotting the words: 'No money is hidden in this hole.' Immediately, he knew that Juk had buried the ten baht there, so he dug up the hole, pocketed the money, and filled the hole back in. Fearing that he'd be found out, he pondered what to do. Then he bent down and wrote in the dirt covering the hole: 'Klae didn't steal the money.'

"When Juk returned for the money, he saw Klae's note and figured out right away that it had been Klae who had stolen the ten baht."

It was Dum who told the kids this story. Afterward, they tried to decide who was smarter, Juk or Klae. They had a heated debate as they strolled over to the grocery to buy themselves some snacks. As they approached the store, Jua, wanting to have his money ready, pulled it out of his pocket. But he wasn't on guard, and the ten-baht coin was snatched right out of his hand.

It was Od who'd nabbed Jua's coin. He held it up high and said to Jua, "Just let me borrow it—you can have it back later." Od suggested the whole gang play a game of hide-the-coin. Jua was frowning, but he didn't have the guts to stand up to Od, who was a lot bigger, so he grudgingly went along.

Curious, a group of girls that was watching TV at the grocery turned to watch. Eventually, they came over to see what the boys were up to. Only Penporn hung back, absorbed in the television and not to be distracted by anything else in the world.

Chong saw the kids assembled over by the sandpit. There'd be a 'Hooray!' and then a 'Yippee!' Even Penporn took her eyes off the TV to see what was happening. And then, as if she were hypnotized, her gaze latched onto something outside as it had been latched onto the TV, and her body moved toward it, getting up and walking on its own, as if defenseless against some unknown force. From the sound of it, the boys were having a great time. Shortly thereafter, Penporn returned to the store, bought herself a candy bar, and went back to watching TV, again cut off from the rest of the world.

Chong had been idly watching. Now, though, he sensed that something had gone wrong. The "hoorays" had turned into squabbling and crying. He saw Jua wiping tears from his face as he hobbled home. Chong couldn't keep still any longer, so he called Kampol over for an interrogation.

"Jua's money got lost," Kampol told him. "Od, Rah, and Chai were playing, hiding Jua's ten-baht coin in a hole in the sand. They'd then dig a bunch of fake holes and have Jua guess the right one. On his first turn, Jua guessed right, so he challenged them to another round. The second time, he guessed right again. So, the third time, Od said everyone—all of us watching—had to close our eyes, too, because people kept staring at the hole with the money, which helped Jua guess the right one. That third turn, Jua didn't get it right. Not on the fourth or fifth times either. Od told him that once he guessed right again, he could have the money back. Jua tried again, and got it wrong again. Then, when Od went to reveal the right hole, there was no money inside. He said it was gone. We dug up all the holes but still couldn't find it."

Chong sent Kampol to go find Jua, and called all the other kids over to the store. With everybody convened, he launched his investigation.

"Everyone else had their eyes closed, Od, except you. And you were the last person to have the coin in his hand, the last to lay eyes on it, and the one who buried the money, isn't that right?"

"Did all of them really have their eyes closed, though?" Od responded. "Maybe someone peeked. Then, after I hid the money, I was busy digging all the other holes so I wasn't paying attention. Someone might have snatched the money while I was doing that."

Chong ordered everyone to empty their pockets and lay out their coins and bills. Most of the kids didn't have any money, though some did. But there was only one person with a ten-baht coin: Rah. Jua bent over the coin to inspect it, but he shook his head, saying no, his ten-baht coin had been much newer than that one. Then Chong suddenly realized: Penporn had used a ten-baht coin to pay for a candy bar after she came back from watching them play!

"I got it!" Chong announced excitedly to everyone. "It must have been Pen. She just paid me for a candy bar with a ten-baht coin. I remember—I gave her back five."

"Nah, Hia Chong," Penporn's older sister Ploy said. "Pen had a ten-baht coin, too. Granny gave her one this morning."

"Well, in that case, the money couldn't have gone anywhere. It must just be buried somewhere in the sand."

Chong found a sieve, shovel, and bucket, and everyone swarmed the sandpit. The kids threw themselves into the task of shoveling and sifting and were having a blast. Chong stood by, watching them work. Suddenly, Penporn was standing next to him. She still had the five-baht coin he had given to her in change held tightly in her fist. He leaned down and told her to put the money in her pocket so it wouldn't get lost. As she slid it into her pocket he heard the clink of coins.

Chong's ears perked up. He laughed to himself, but didn't let on. At that moment a customer happened to be calling for him from in front of the shop, so he hustled back. When he returned again, he jumped in and helped the children.

Finally, a ten-baht coin was caught by the sieve. It came up in some sand scooped by Chong. The children were as thrilled as can be. None of them had noticed that Penporn had disappeared. Chong scanned the neighborhood with his eyes, trying to find her. He finally saw the little girl moving toward something as though a force were drawing her to it. She stopped in front of an oleander bush, where a large caterpillar clung to a chewed-up flower.

Studying the creature, Penporn was not to be distracted by anything else in the world. And the rest of the world took no note of her comings and goings either.

Our House

Kampol and Oan shared one dream: they wanted a tree house of their own. They'd gotten the idea for it from an American movie they saw on TV. Of course, they kept it a secret. Only when they were alone did they talk about their dream house, and even then they spoke in whispers.

In the mornings before they went to school, the two would stop under the poinciana, gaze up into its great big branches, and picture their fort. For several days, the two boys, their eyes full of hope, had been scavenging the neighborhood for miscellaneous scrap materials. They skipped nothing. Whatever they happened to turn up, that object instantly revealed itself as a potential component of their little house. They dragged all manner of odds and ends over and piled them next to a bush behind Mrs. Tongjan's house. No one could figure out how they would turn all that clutter into anything. But the two of them had precise plans—from the materials they'd gathered, they'd already developed a clear mental image of the house.

But the next step had them dismayed. They couldn't figure out how to actually build the fort. Where should they even start? Plus, they needed to be up in the tree to do the construction. They could climb the poinciana when they had their hands free, without any building materials, and all they could do once they got up there was sit in the fork, hugging the trunk. In the tree, they would dream and dream until they tired themselves out, and then they would climb down. In their scheming they focused on Chong, as a person they trusted to help them.

The next night, Kampol and Oan, newly even more hopeless, commiserated over their situation. They had placed their trust in the wrong person. They had allowed Chong in on their secret, but he crushed their dream. When they had brought him to the tree to show him, his expression was still optimistic and enthusiastic. But once he saw their pile of building materials, Chong just shook his head. No matter how desperately the two of them begged, Chong just said it was impossible, and stuck to that. The two kids got mad at him, wanting to preserve their dream. As deflated as they were, they were not going to give up.

On their way home from school one day, Kampol and Oan passed a junk shop. They both slowed down at the same time. Hearts thumping, they stopped and stared: a giant cardboard box just the size of the house they'd been picturing was sitting on the bed of a pickup truck in the parking lot. Heightwise, it came up to the chin of the adult who was next to it. The man was reaching into the box and pulling out bundle after bundle of mixed paper. When he couldn't reach any more of them, he tipped the box over, ducked low, and went into the box to get the remaining bundles. The shop owner was looking at the scale and scribbled in his ledger. Finally, the giant box was placed on the scale, too. Money in hand, the man pulled off in his pickup truck. Kampol and Oan dug in their pockets, pooled their money together, and counted it up. Then they marched into the shop like they were important customers.

Oan was in the front and Kampol was in the back—the box balanced on their heads. Their yelps and laughter resounded all the way to who-knows-where. Chong ran out of his store to see when he heard them.

The "house" was dropped onto its side in the middle of the neighborhood's vacant lot. The bottom of the box, which was taped shut, faced west, while the "door" opened to the east. When they tried going inside, they saw that they could easily lie down side by side—it didn't feel cramped at all. The two agreed that they would take turns watching over their fort. Oan went home to change and then came back to do his homework in their new house. Kampol changed, too, went over and gave Dang his massage, and then came back to do his homework in their new house as well. Everyone who passed by ducked low to look inside and say hello. Their friends gave them envious side eyes. Jua came over and hung out by the entrance. Mon called the two new homeowners for dinner, but they yelled back that they weren't hungry because they didn't want to abandon the house. Eventually, she had to deliver plates of food to them there. The two boys were completely caught up in the world of their new house, opening the door one minute and closing it the next.

That evening, Oan went back to his old house. He rummaged around until he found a candle. Mon had him stand it up inside a glass and lit it for him, and now their new house glimmered through the cracks around the door. When the candle burned low, Kampol ran over to fetch pillows and a blanket. Tonight, they thought, they would sleep in their new home for the first time…but their plan was foiled.

"Put those pillows back," Mon told Kampol sternly. "And go get Oan. Playtime's over."

Kampol delivered the bad news to his friend, but Oan refused to leave. The two of them mulled over what to do about the fact that Mon wouldn't let them spend the night in their new house. They hadn't come up with a solution yet when someone's hand opened the door. Noi poked his face in. Their hearts sank. But before they managed to say a thing, they heard Mon yelling at them from afar.

"Your mama's calling you," Noi said.

"Let's bring it with us and put it inside the house for now," Kampol said to Oan.

Noi quickly chimed in, "How the hell are you going to get it in there? It's wider than the front door. Just leave it. I'll sleep here and guard it for you. Come out! Your mama's coming this way with her cane, you see her?"

Kampol and Oan dragged themselves out and Noi crawled in, taking their place. It pained them terribly to leave, but they didn't dare put up a fight. Noi shut the door.

"That bastard gets one night, that's it," Oan said to Kampol in the dark as they lay on their mattress in the house.

"Tomorrow's Friday. Before school, we should leave it with Hia Chong."

"This weekend, we'll spend both days at our fort."

"I think at night we should carry it over and put it in front of your house. Your mama probably won't mind if we sleep right outside."

The two of them chatted until late. Once they fell asleep, they were dead asleep. Even as the next day broke, they were oblivious to the heavy rainstorm that had passed through during the night. Noi had bailed out of the little house hours ago. It had drunk up the water like a sponge. All it took were three nudges of the westerly wind, and the fort fell flat on its belly.

Liberty Beach

Most of the children didn't have very much pocket money. Therefore, they managed their finances with prudence, but the hour just after school was when they blissfully ignored their budgets. Just outside the fence of the Baan Huaykapi School was a parking lot where, among parents in their cars or trucks or on their motorbikes waiting to pick up their children, trailers and pushcarts offered snacks and toys. Some of the kids were willing to forego candy and peanuts and such at lunchtime in order to save their money and buy goodies after school. The ones who'd spent their money would throw tantrums at the parents who had come to pick them up. Some of those parents, though, could only shake their heads with eyes that were more disappointed than their children's.

One day, Kampol, munching on some prawn chips, saw how all the other children had boundaries imposed on them. Without knowing why exactly, he suddenly felt superior.

"Not having parents isn't all bad," Kampol told Oan as they walked home.

"Why not?" Oan asked him.

"I have more freedom than other people, that's why. I don't have to keep asking my mama for money. I can buy all the snacks I want, I can play wherever I want; I don't have to ask permission from anybody."

Oan thought for a moment, then asked, "But…what if you run out of money?"

"If I run out of money, I just go give Uncle Dang a massage, or I fetch people when they have phone calls."

It was true that since the start of the term, Kampol had pocket money for school every day. A stomach and face pinched by hunger wasn't something he'd had to endure, not really. His means of earning money evolved as he went along, but the amount was rather steady. Dang, the man who needed massages, was his number one source of income. Then there was his post staffing the telephone, notifying people when they had calls. He also did whatever general tasks people from Mrs. Tongjan's neighborhood hired him for.

"But what if Uncle Dang doesn't want a massage, no calls come in, no one needs anything from the store, and you've got no money?"

"Then I'd go find some other job, obviously. I can do anything I want, go anywhere I want."

"And where would you go? You don't have the nerve to go anywhere."

"You want to bet? I could take off now if I wanted," Kampol said, his voice cracking. "You want to come? Anywhere—the flea market, Ang Sila, even all the way to Bang Saen—any place is a possibility."

"You'd dare to go all the way to Bang Saen by yourself? Do you even know how to get there?"

"Piece of cake. It's the red *songthaew* bus. To get to Ang Sila is the blue one. They take you right there."

Consequently, Oan went home by himself. Kampol, meanwhile, boarded the red bus to Bang Saen.

He hadn't meant for it to happen, but here he was, in Nong Mon, because of his bragging. All the other passengers got off the bus. The famous Nong Mon market was bustling, the shops along its front forming a long golden trail of lights. The bus stayed a while—the driver calling for passengers who wanted to go to Bang Saen Beach. Eventually, it pulled out. Alone, Kampol shrank in his seat on the cushioned bench. His legs trembled; he was rattled.

He had felt lonesome before, many times in fact. But in those moments, even if he didn't have anyone in the world, he had his familiar neighborhood, with its familiar crevices and corners that he knew so well, which provided comfort. There was the wall outside Chong's shop, where the jasmine bush stood, marked with dirt from where he leaned against it when he visited. Or there was the wedged fork of the poinciana. Or behind Mrs. Tongjan's house, his hideout beneath the shrub whose leafy branches bowed down and kissed the ground. When desolation struck, Kampol had these familiar nooks to embrace him.

Kampol pushed the button to indicate he wanted the stop at the beachfront. He saw the ocean; he'd now seen Bang Saen. But his courage had snuck off someplace he couldn't follow. The sea was dark and the beach was black; how ugly they were. In the murky sky, the sun faded behind a cluster of clouds. Far off there were people walking, but only a few. Kampol was hunched forward, weighed down by the backpack strapped on his back. His large eyes grew sad and his eyebrows hung. He looked left and right as he took short little leaden steps along the road that bordered the beach. He'd made it to Bang Saen, all by himself. But this place had nothing that appealed to him. None of it made him feel like he was having fun. So, he went to wait for the bus to take him back home—or, even if it wasn't a home, it was at least his turf.

Kampol waited…

A bus apparently wasn't easy to come by in Bang Saen in the middle of a weekday. They didn't come all the way down to the beachfront if there weren't passengers who wanted to come from Nong Mon. With no buses coming in, there were none departing either. The one that had brought Kampol had already headed back.

The sun showed itself again briefly, before truly departing. Kampol no longer cared what kind of vehicle the headlights were coming from, he flagged every one that went by. But the cars and pickup trucks simply zoomed past him.

When a bus finally pulled in to pick him up, its lights washed over him, shining on the tears that glistened all over his face. His mouth was wide and his entire body jerked with each sniffle. When he stepped onto the bus, a pair of passengers, a man and a woman, noticed him. Together they tried relentlessly to get a word out of him. Kampol ignored them the whole way. At most he nodded or shook his head. But, thanks to them, he cheered up and stopped crying. When he saw the TrueWare sign, he beamed and quickly rang the bell.

"He's back!" Oan shouted at the top of his lungs. "There's no need to go after him, Hia Chong."

Seeing his friends lined up waiting for him at the entrance to their housing community, Kampol grinned wide, with all of his teeth on display. Chong let out a sigh and walked away without so much as a word to Kampol. His friends squealed, surrounding him from all sides. Kampol, feeling grand and glorious, told them about his adventure, laughing louder than anyone.

Crickets

Mr. Sanya, one of Kampol's teachers, lived in a house behind the school, and he sent Kampol to fetch his sneakers,
which he'd forgotten right outside his front door. Kampol
had the shoes when he heard something, his ears pricking
up. He turned left and right, trying to locate the source of
the sound. He found a pile of cardboard and Styrofoam boxes
and wooden crates—all full of crickets. Each container was
covered with a plastic net and tied tightly with rope. Kampol
put his face right up to one of the boxes. The many, many
crickets were either perched on or crawled over cardboard egg
trays. In one corner of the box was a dish of water and a dish
of what was likely food, but he couldn't tell what kind exactly.

Kampol brought Mr. Sanya his sneakers; he was playing
kick volleyball with the gym teacher, Mr. Somkiat. While Mr.
Sanya was changing shoes, Kampol stood right next to him,
refusing to leave.

"Mr. Sanya," Kampol said. The teacher looked up with
one eyebrow raised, implying, "Yes?" "Why do you have all
those crickets?"

"Oh, I farm them to sell. A man comes for them every
few months, after they've reproduced enough to fill up the

boxes." Mr. Sanya eyed Kampol with a little smile. "If you want to try raising some, get a big box ready this evening. Tomorrow after school I'll give you two pairs of males and females."

Kampol was on cloud nine. Not only did he find a large box, but he even went to the grocery store in the older housing development to ask for any spare egg trays. He also found a plastic net behind Jua's house, but when he wouldn't say what he wanted the net for, Jua refused to let him have it. In the end, in exchange for the net, he had to tell his secret. He also had to give his word that once his crickets mated, he would give Jua a pair.

Kampol monitored the crickets very closely. Their food looked like chicken feed—Mr. Sanya let Kampol buy five baht's worth of it from his own supply. But crickets were too easy to keep. Kampol didn't have to do a thing. All he really did was stare at them, which he did relentlessly. His four crickets looked so much alike that he couldn't tell them apart at first, but with perseverance, he could eventually distinguish all of them. He gave them names to have something to call them by. The first pair he named after his parents, Ratom and Namfon, despite the fact that his name meant "misery" and hers meant "rain." Both names seemed rather odd now that he thought about them given that their family name meant "bright." Later on, when the two crickets he'd named after his parents had children, he wanted to call them Boy and Jon. As for the other pair, he named them Somdej and Somrak, after two of his classmates who were always getting teased by their homeroom teacher for being boyfriend and girlfriend. Kampol was thinking ahead: the idea was that when crickets Somdej and Somrak had children, he would ask his two friends to help him name the offspring.

When he went to school, he left his cricket box with Chong. And as soon as school let out, he ran home without even waiting for Oan. Even when he was eating or doing his homework, the cricket box stood right next to him. On weekends, he didn't play with his friends. He poured his heart and soul into watching the crickets, waiting for the moment he would get to see the children of Ratom, Namfon, Somdej, and Somrak. And Kampol wasn't the only one. A constant stream of his friends stopped by to check on them. Everybody said that when the new crickets were born, they wanted to buy a pair.

But once the nymphs had hatched and were bouncing around in the box, Kampol told his friends that he couldn't sell any of them just yet. Mr. Sanya had told him that you had to wait until the crickets grew a bit before you could tell if they were male or female. His eager friends could only bide their time. But even after the crickets had grown, Kampol continued to give them the runaround, drumming up one excuse after another. Jua was the only one whom Kampol gave a pair of nymphs.

The crickets chirped loudly inside the box. At first Kampol named every single one of them. Of course, there was Boy and Jon. He thought they had grown enough that he was able to tell them apart, but within minutes of their christening, Boy and Jon started hopping around and Kampol lost track of them. After that, he was reluctant to make a definitive call as to which crickets were Boy and Jon because he worried that he would mistake new ones for the originals.

"How many crickets have you got, Kampol?" Mr. Sanya asked him one morning. "The buyer's coming next week."

Kampol felt his heart stop. He stood numb and unspeaking.

"Well, maybe you should hold off on selling them. You don't have that many yet. It's better if you keep them for breeding—does that sound like a plan? Or would you prefer to sell now?"

Kampol looked down. "Yes, I think it's better for me to keep them for now."

That same day, at Chong's shop, while Kampol's orchestra of crickets trilled noisily in the back, Dum and Gaew, Tongbai's husband, were bantering over glasses of whiskey at the terrazzo table just outside.

"People eat them. You can toast them like grasshoppers. But they're tastier," Dum said.

"Nah, people aren't going to get into it. They feel different. People want to be rid of grasshoppers, which eat all the crops, so people eat them just to be done with them. But crickets make a nice sound. They're too lovable to be food. When people farm them it's for animal feed."

"Oh Gaew, you've been living under a rock. A couple of days ago, I was watching that show *Fight Hard and Get Rich*. They went to talk to someone who farms crickets and delivers them to restaurants. Right on camera, they threw them in a wok and fried them up. Not only that, but they gave a ton of recipes for them that sounded amazing. Stay right there, I'll prove it to you," Dum said, and then he walked over to Chong.

That afternoon, Kampol hurried back to the store as usual. As soon as he arrived, he made a beeline for the back of the shop. He lifted up his cricket box—but it was silent. Right at that moment, Chong happened to notice him.

"Oh, Boy, you're back. I sold those crickets for you. At first, I didn't think there were that many, but I counted them up and there were actually forty-eight. I got a baht apiece for them. Here, Uncle Dum gave you fifty."

Kampol felt like he'd been gut-punched. He heard Dum call him over, urging him to come have a taste. He walked woodenly over to the table. His family was lying on the plate, some face up, some face down, their limbs all mixed together. Suddenly, Dum grabbed one and held it right in front of his face—it was Papa! And Mama was about to go in Gaew's mouth! His friends Somdej and Somrak had probably already been eaten. As for Boy and Jon… He couldn't even recognize himself. He couldn't tell if he'd already been eaten.

Birthday Parties

There was a party over at the big house to celebrate Mrs. Tongjan's sixtieth birthday. All of her relatives, young and old, even some of them from other provinces, turned up early in the morning to wish her a happy birthday. When they stepped out of their cars, they were all bearing gifts.

Mrs. Tongjan, dressed in red Thai silk, greeted each of her guests out front. They waied her with their palms joined, and she returned the gesture, ushering them inside the house. The presents were left on a large table outside, and under the shade of the fragrant ylang-ylang tree, a long table was overflowing with an impressive array of food.

Because Mrs. Tongjan's yard didn't have a fence, the children found themselves standing in a group, able to steal glances from close range. To them, though, both the food and the gifts seemed so, so far away. They didn't realize it, but they kept drifting closer. And closer. Nobody was outside. From inside the house came the humming sound of prayers; monks had been invited to come and bless the special occasion. The children inched toward the tables—to the point where, were they to stretch their arms out, they would be able to touch the food.

They realized that they had drawn too near only after the chanting died down. That's when the sounds of movement began to pick up from inside the house. The children began to retreat just as party guests were funneling out. For a moment, Mrs. Tongjan's family members stared, surprised, over the spread of food to the group of dark, dirty children. From their side of the table, Kampol, Oan, Jua, Noi, Rah, Chai, and Od stared back over the food at the handsomely dressed crowd with awe. They had no choice but to concede that they must step back further and make way for that cleanliness and the resplendence, for the deliciousness, for opportunity and good fortune…would such things, they wondered, trickle down to them one day?

Now that the ceremony was finished, the party got underway. When it got to the point where guests were starting to help themselves to food, Noi was struck by a moment of clarity: "Let's get out of here. It's pathetic to stand around watching people eat." The others snapped back to their senses, too, and they all felt embarrassed, so they tore themselves away by turning around and heading to their hangout under the poinciana. There, they found the girls sitting in a circle playing jacks.

"I want a birthday party, too," Jua said.

"I've never had a birthday party in my life," Kampol remarked.

"Me neither," Oan said. "My mama neither, nor my papa."

"If I had the money, I'd have a huge birthday party. I'd get a cake this big," Noi said, spreading his arms as wide as a washtub, "and eat the whole thing myself."

"What about the people who brought you presents? Aren't you at least going to give them a slice?" Ploy asked.

"Who said I was going to invite anyone?" Noi said.

"Okay. Then if I ever have a birthday party, you're not invited."

"Don't forget to invite me!" Kampol and Jua said almost at the same time. Ploy nodded at them.

"I don't give a damn about having a birthday party. It's boring," Chai said. "Last year, my papa had one for me." The announcement caused a stir among the friends, all of them wanting to know how big the cake was. "There wasn't any cake. There was only papaya salad, *larb*, and *koi*. My papa invited his friends from the factory, and they stayed up partying until dawn."

Since there was no cake to talk about, his friends—it was obvious from their expressions—lost interest.

"I want to have a birthday party, but the kind with a cake."

"Hmm…"

"Hey, look!" Rah said and pointed at the garbage can at the base of the utility pole in front of Mrs. Tongjan's house, into which someone was dumping some trash.

But to the children, the stuff was not trash. Rah, Chai, and the twins, Gae and Gay, scampered over as the other children cheered them on.

They returned with armloads of crumpled and torn wrapping paper. Gay discovered two birthday cards within the ball of paper she'd snagged, so she read them aloud:

"'Dear Mother, wishing you make it to a ripe old age full of health, happiness, and comfort. You should know that I'll always love and respect you deeply, and may we enjoy many more decades together.' Oh, that's well put. This one says, 'Have a happy, happy birthday, Grandma!' That's it…pretty short if you ask me. He should have written more."

Because they all wanted to have a birthday party, the kids

went down the list to see who in the neighborhood was having their birthday next, in case they could all chip in for a cake and throw a party for once.

Two days later, Old Noi, bent over her cane, came to Chong's shop with Penporn hanging onto her blouse.

"Can you help me? The kids said this afternoon, after they come home from school, they want to throw me a birthday party. This morning they all gave me birthday messages they'd written for me, but I couldn't read any of them since, as you know, I don't know how to read. I had to have Jai read them to me. But there's still this one left, from the little one here—she wrote it all on her own. Jai said he couldn't make out what it says. I had Dum look at it, too, and he said she wrote it so small that he can't read it either."

Chong took the piece of paper and looked at it. It was some of the wrapping paper, which had been cut into a rectangle. On the back of it were three rows of round, long squiggles, all squished together. Chong pretended to read it aloud:

"Happy birthday, Grandma Noi. Wishing you lots of happiness, good health, and ten thousand more years of life!"

Old Noi bobbed her head, looking pleased. When Chong asked, "Did I read that right?" Penporn nodded with a tight-lipped smile, her eyes shining.

Old Noi hugged her granddaughter and said, "Aw, she sure can write."

Fads

When the rubber-band fad swept through the school, all over the playground or anywhere there was open space in the morning before class, during lunchtime, recess, and after school, girls were executing sideways jumps over long ropes made from the bands and boys were bent over with their butts sticking up in the air, each blowing on a band on the ground, trying to land it on his opponent's. Shorts and skirt pockets were stuffed full of the bands, which, of course, didn't simply take over the school but followed the kids home as well. When the craze finally began to fizzle, the kids started talking about bouncy balls. Eventually, Auntie Nian, who ran the toy store, took down her rubber-band display board and stored it away.

New trends had a way of barreling in. Seemingly while Kampol was still bent over practicing his aim with his rubber band, around him the world had already moved on. Little rubber balls, in a rainbow of colorful patterns, were now bouncing up and down all over the school. That afternoon, Kampol headed over to Auntie Nian's shop. He had to purchase five baht's worth of snacks to get one bouncy ball as a free gift. You couldn't choose which design you got, so the kids were always showing off the styles they had in their collections. Kampol spent his money on snacks every day, getting one more bouncy ball every day, one new pattern a day, to add to his collection—except on the not-infrequent days when the designs repeated. Morning, noon, and night, bouncy balls were brought out of pockets for showdowns. The owners weren't always able to chase down their runaway balls, and often a bunch of kids dove in a pile, thinking the same one looked like it could be theirs.

Kampol went to school with his pockets bulging with bouncy balls. But one morning, everywhere at school, the world had begun to move on again. Bouncy balls were being edged out by modeling clay. For the boys, the battleground was any smooth concrete surface. One kid would pinch off a thumb-sized piece, raise his hand real high, and fling the bit of modeling clay onto the ground. His opponent would take a chunk of equal size and take aim at the first player's blob. A hit meant the pieces were his for the taking. Whoever ran out of modeling clay but still wanted to play had to rush over to Auntie Nian's shop and buy some more. Those with good aim could, on a given day, earn themselves a fairly large clump of the clay. The goal was to own a ball that resembled a globe, created from winning and combining nuggets of different colors. Kampol, in his unremitting desire to keep up with trends, was forced to empty the bouncy balls from his pockets into his school bag and procure himself some modeling clay. He won some and lost some, but eventually he had a sizable hunk. He was zealous about honing his skills. At home, he played against Oan. They were evenly matched and basically took turns winning and losing.

Then came the next fad. Kampol, with the big blob of

modeling clay still protruding from the pocket of his shorts, watched as the older kids practiced with their yo-yos, winding the string, thrusting it out, and reeling it back. This time, he felt oddly fed up by the whole rigmarole and didn't hurry right over to Auntie Nian's store to buy a yo-yo, but he also didn't pull out his modeling clay for a game. That whole day, Kampol watched the others playing, some with yo-yos, some with modeling clay, but he didn't have the slightest desire to join in. He was sick and tired of all of it.

That Saturday, outside Chong's shop, Oan and Jua were in the middle of a modeling clay battle. Kampol, sullen, watched from afar. He flipped his palm over and glanced at the hunk in his hand, but that was all he did. Chong, who'd been reading, put his book down on the table and walked over to him.

"What's the matter, Boy? Why aren't you playing with your friends?"

"They'll get bored of it in no time. Give it two more days, Hia Chong, and nobody's going to be playing with modeling clay anymore."

"What makes you say that? All I see all day is you kids going crazy hurling that stuff around. Why do you think everybody's going to give it up all of a sudden?"

"Before we got into modeling clay, do you remember what we were into?"

"Hmm…I can't remember anymore."

"It was bouncy balls. Don't you remember that time one of my balls bounced into your water glass?"

"Oh, right. Bouncy balls were everywhere!"

"Yeah. And before bouncy balls, it was rubber bands. Before that it was something else—and on and on. We got bored of them and move on to something else."

"Well, who's to blame for that? You all are the ones who lose interest."

"I don't lose interest. I never got bored by any of it. When we were playing with the rubber bands, I'd just gotten myself a good one. Then all of a sudden, everybody else switched to playing with bouncy balls. And then when I almost had a ball with every pattern, they moved on to modeling clay. And now that I'm good with my shots, they're about to move on to something else again. You just watch, Hia Chong, in two days no one's going to be playing with it anymore. They're already starting to practice with yo-yos. I'm sick of it. I don't want to learn how to yo-yo like the rest of them fools."

"Hmm…interesting. So, does this mean you haven't lost interest in modeling clay or that you've lost interest in everything?"

"It's just how everybody starts playing something, and then they get tired of it and quit. Even when I'm not bored of it yet, I have to quit along with them, too. I'm bored by them—that's what it is."

"Who's 'them'? If you're not bored by the game, why do you have to follow what they do and stop? Can't you do your own thing and just keep playing? Who are these 'them' anyway?"

"'Them' is everybody—at school and here, too. If they're not playing what I want to play anymore, then who am I supposed to play with?"

"And you can't play by yourself…hmm. And the yo-yos, you really aren't tempted to get one like the others are doing?"

"It's not that. It's just that I know they'll end up getting tired of the yo-yos in no time, too."

Chong chuckled. "All right, I have an idea. I've been in this situation before. Really, when I was your age, I once refused to do things the way everybody else did them. I got really fed up and found myself a toy I could play with alone."

"What was your toy? What did you play?"

"My toy…my toy was books. Books can be fun and you don't need anybody to play."

"Boy, your papa's here! Hurry! He brought the big water truck, too!" Oan and Jua screamed.

Kampol ran out. The truck was parked in front of the grocery. Wasu opened the door to let his son climb up and put Boy on his lap. Kampol shouted toward the store, "I'm going to go play with my papa. I'll see you tomorrow, Hia Chong."

Chong sighed. Picking up his book, he went back to playing alone.

Backup Strategy

Kampol and Jua were learning to play checkers. In front of the grocery was a terrazzo game table. The two of them arranged their bottle caps—Kampol's were face down and Jua's were face up—and wasted no time making their moves. They each charged ahead, only caring about capturing their opponent's checkers and paying absolutely no attention to defending their own. But, as reckless as they were, neither was managing to make a single jump, not even when their pieces were all mixed together across the board.

Eventually—and around the same time—both Kampol and Jua reached the opposite side of the board with a piece and was crowned king, and neither had lost a single piece to the other. They kept on playing, earning several more kings each, but still they hadn't taken out a single one of the other's checkers. Jua grew frustrated; Kampol sensed that something was off.

"Hia Chong," Kampol yelled, "can you come have a look? What do we have to do to jump each other's pieces?"

Chong was in the middle of grabbing something for a customer. "Well, you've just got to try," he hollered from inside. "Or else you have to be willing to trade—sacrifice one of yours first in order to get one in return."

Kampol and Jua both stared at their checkers, trying to plot out a trade. It was Kampol's turn, but he still couldn't figure out a way to let Jua jump one of his.

"Hia Chong," Kampol yelled again, "I don't even see how to give up one of mine. Can you please come look? How do I do it?"

"Do it with any of them. Move one of your pieces right up to one of his and just let him jump you. And if there's one where if he makes a jump, you can do it back, then that's the best," Chong yelled from behind his desk in the back of the store.

Kampol studied his checkers for a long time. "Hia Chong," he called again, "there's no way."

"Just move whichever one, and soon enough something will get jumped!"

Kampol simply moved at random. Jua stared at the board for a long time, trying to find a way to sacrifice one of his in a trade, but no matter how long he stared, none of his checkers presented itself as a candidate.

"Hia Chong," Jua called, "can you *please* come look? I don't see how to make a jump happen no matter what I do."

Chong closed his ledger, got up from his desk with a sigh, and came over to the terrazzo table. Arms crossed, he inspected the situation on the board. Then he laughed, shaking his head side to side, a bit exasperated.

"You two are really something—Jua, you're using the white squares and Boy's using the black ones. Play like that and it's impossible for there to ever be a way to jump. No wonder you've been having such a hard time capturing each other's pieces," Chong said. Then he cleared the board and re-arranged the pieces so the kids could start again. "Remember that you have to set them up this way. If you put them on the white squares, you both have to do white. Or if you put them on black, you both have to do black. All right...this time you'll definitely get to make some jumps."

Kampol and Jua returned to playing, and Chong went back to his desk. The two boys made their moves quietly; only every so often would a bit of their conversation be faintly audible. At first, they were hypervigilant, scared of losing one of their men. But then they ran into the same problem again. Unbelievably, despite the pieces being set up properly, they still couldn't capture each other's men.

"Hia Chong!" Jua hollered. "Can you come look? Boy won't let me jump one of his."

"Why don't *you* sacrifice one of yours first?" Kampol asked.

"All right, all right. Don't argue," Chong yelled from his desk. "It's good that you're defending your pieces. When you have nowhere else to move, you'll have no choice but to give one up anyway."

The boys continued playing, both frowning.

"What are you dodging away for?" Kampol growled, but not too loudly.

"Well what are you dodging away for?" Jua snapped right back, also keeping his voice down.

"Because you did first."

"No, you did. A bunch of times now, too."

"What's going on?" Chong said, sounding annoyed. "Can't you two just play in peace?"

"Come look, Hia Chong. Jua won't let himself be jumped. He keeps dodging me!"

"He's complaining about me, but he's doing the same thing!"

Chong stood up, huffing loudly through his nose. He

walked back over to the terrazzo table to investigate the situation. From the look of things, he didn't see any issues. Both sides, face up and face down, were at dead ends. Each of them had only one possible move left, and once it was made, that checker was as good as captured. It was only a matter of whose turn was next.

"Go on, make a move. Let's see if it's really true that no one can jump," Chong said. Kampol reached for the checker that Chong had his eye on.

"Wait! What are you doing?" Chong cried. "You can't move backward! That's why neither one of you has managed to capture a single piece." He scratched his head, then sat down, ordering the opponents to start again.

At long last, the first game of checkers came to an end. Jua was whooping because he had won. Kampol, on the other hand, crinkled his brow and refused to play anymore.

"I'm not playing," Kampol said petulantly. "Hia Chong, you only gave Jua tips—if I had known this was going to happen, I would have kept playing the old way." His large eyes reddened and welled up.

Jua laughed and taunted him: "Loser! Crybaby!"

A blasé look on his face, Chong cast his eyes toward the sky, where gray clouds were rolling in from a distance.

The Wedding

Jua's uncle Berm came over to consult Jua's grandfather, Old Jai, about a terrible predicament he had found himself in.

"I really didn't mean for this to happen, Papa, I swear," Berm said, his face a picture of torment. "She and I are friends. The girl I like is actually a friend of hers. Papa, what do I do now? I didn't mean for this to happen, really."

"Well, don't do anything. Just sit tight," his father replied, rolling himself a cigarette, completely unperturbed.

"I can't sit tight anymore, Papa. She's already four months pregnant. She wants me to go ask her parents for her hand. Her parents are insisting on forty thousand baht, but then they'll take care of the wedding, that's what they said."

"Are you sure it's your kid? You're positive you're the only one she's slept with?"

"I'm sure I'm not, but she says that I was the only one she got in bed with around that time."

"You idiot! She didn't get knocked up sleeping with other men, but she did with you? Why didn't you use protection? With a stupid mistake like that, you deserve what happened."

"Yeah, Papa, that…she intentionally trapped me. My friend told me she's had her eye on me for ages, even though she knew I was going out with her friend. It was New Year's Eve when it all went down. I got smashed early in the night. I couldn't even tell you what time it was when I went into the bedroom to sleep. Sometime around midnight, all my friends decided to go to the temple and get blessed with holy water. Nobody woke me up. If they had none of this would've happened. Only when they were on their way back from the temple did they realize that she wasn't with them. They looked and looked for her and still couldn't find her. Close to dawn, one of my friends came into the room where I was to sleep. When he opened the door, there she was… So everybody found out, and there was no way to deny it. Papa, what do I do? I really don't want to get married."

"It's up to you. If you don't want to get married, then don't get married."

"That's not an option, Papa. They said that if I don't do the right thing, they're going to send someone to shoot me in the head."

So Berm didn't have any choice but to get married. But there was still haggling to be done over the price of the dowry. Ultimately, the bride's family offered a compromise of twenty thousand, but they had to hand over the whole forty first, and the bride's family would give back half after the wedding.

On the day of the nuptials, no one was more excited than Jua, the groom's nephew. He put on a new shirt and a new pair of shorts; it was only a shame he didn't have shoes. Kampol and Oan—though they had no business lining up with the family—were there, dressed in their school uniforms, which were best clothes. Old Jai's friends and family had gathered early in the morning to walk with the *khan maak* bowl over to the bride's home, which was in town.

Among those in the khan maak procession, there was

one other person without shoes, Old Gan, Jua's grandpa's dearest friend. Now elderly, the two of them had been buddies since they were young men and had never grown even an inch apart. Normally, both of them sported fisherman's pants, secured with a simple tuck at the waist, and nothing else. They hadn't worn shirts or shoes for years and years. But for this affair, they had to show Jai's son's auspicious occasion due respect. The two old pals, therefore, were dressed in brand-new long-sleeved shirts and long pants—their outfits matched in cut and color from head to toe, as if they were twins. The biggest challenge for them, though, was wearing shoes. They had both tried on several pairs in various styles. Ultimately, they'd settled on a pair of flip-flops for each of them. Even still, Jai was the only one who could endure keeping them on. Old Gan carried the shoes in his hand the entire time.

Outside of the bride's home, they finished assembling the khan maak procession. With three long "Ho's!" and three quick "Hew's!" the wedding parade began marching. Jua, Kampol, and Oan walked on ahead of the groom. As they neared the foot of the stairs leading into the house, the scene turned chaotic. Berm stood there in his suit, looking pale and like his saliva was too thick to swallow. He leaned down and whispered to Kampol:

"Boy, go inside the house and ask for the bride. Tell her Berm is begging—would it be okay if there were only three of the gold and silver gates? I didn't prepare enough envelopes. Hurry!"

Kampol sprinted off immediately. Before long, he reported back:

"The mother of the bride said you can just hand out the cash without putting it into the envelopes. Her relatives don't mind."

Berm, Old Jai, and Old Gan put their heads together for a moment. Then the khan maak procession went ahead. When they reached the first symbolic gate, blocked by a gold chain, Berm took out some envelopes. He made it through that first obstacle, then the second one, and then the third. Now he had run out of the six envelopes he had prepared, and his hands were empty in his pockets. Ahead, nearly ten more gates, barred by gold chains remained. The groom smiled nervously at the bride's relatives, who were holding firm at their stations and keeping the chains taut.

"Ready?" you could hear Old Gan asking, to which Old Jai replied, "Let's do it." The entire procession plowed ahead hard, hoping to propel the groom through the gates one way or another. The bride's relatives, not to be outdone, fought back, defending their stations as if their lives depended on it. The two sides pushed back and forth and back and forth for some time, but neither gave ground. Then a command came from Old Jai: "Wait! Retreat for now! Back!"

The khan maak unit retreated. The groom's suit was crumpled all over. The children, who had jumped way out of the way, came back, sheepishly watching the situation.

"Let's go home, Papa," Berm said. "If they won't let us through, we don't have to go through."

"No, no. That would be a disgrace, son," Old Gan said. Then he threw his flip-flops on the ground. He stripped off his shirt, which was drenched in sweat, wrapped it around his head, snatched up his shoes again, and squeezed them, determined. "Round two. Let's go."

The groom's team got into ranks and charged again. The children watched from the sidelines, their hearts pounding. This time, the tenacity of the groom's side was intimidating to behold. Some brawny cousins of the bride who had been holding back felt themselves called to duty and rushed in to provide reinforcements. What ensued was a fierce struggle. Jua panicked as he saw his Uncle Berm being swallowed up in the crowd.

But soon enough his uncle was thrust up into the air, his body supported on a bed of hands. You could hear Old Jai counting, "One, two…" When he got to three, Berm glided over the wall of bodies formed by the bride's relatives.

The ceremony was allowed to proceed. The bride and groom first paid respect to their elders, who gave them gifts of money. Then the guests lined up to pour water from the ceremonial conch shell over the couple's hands. The reception was set to begin at noon. At the start of the program, the groom's father and the bride's mother exchanged a few dirty looks over the money gifted to the couple. The bride's mother demanded to keep the money the couple had received from her relatives for herself. The groom's father, on the other hand, said he thought all the money should go to the couple, but if the mother of the bride was going to take that position, then he would claim the money his relatives had given them should be given to him. They didn't argue for long. It was agreed: the bride and groom would have to hand the money from the various relatives over to their parents.

At the lunch reception, the kids brightened up when they saw that they had been allocated an entire table just for them. Kampol, Jua, and Oan were just starting to meet their new friends, and had put only a few bites of food in their mouths, when the bride, in her white dress with her belly slightly protruding, came over to their table. She whispered something to one of the boys. The kid shook his head.

"I don't want to get yelled at. I'm not going over there. Have Tee do it."

The bride looked over at the boy named Tee, who also immediately shook his head. The others all followed suit at once, swinging their heads from side to side.

"One of you, anyone, just go and grab it. Otherwise you won't get to eat," she threatened.

The kids went quiet for a bit, and then one of them stood up. "In that case, I'll go eat in the kitchen." The others stood up after him. Kampol, Jua, and Oan were the only ones left sitting at the table.

"How about you, can you help me, please?" The bride's finger was aimed at Jua. "Just go over to that table and grab the bottle of whiskey for me." She pointed at a table where every seat was occupied, and an untouched bottle of whiskey stood prominently in the middle—she wasn't going to let anyone leave the party with whiskey she'd paid for.

Jua, though dumbstruck, complied. He returned empty-handed, however.

"They told me to come back over here and ask who wants it and what they are going to do with it."

"Tell them Uncle Berm sent you for it," she said.

Jua went again but returned empty-handed again. The bride scowled. She had been watching the entire time and saw how the guests at that table denied the kid the bottle, even though not one of them cared to open it for a drink. The three boys sat in total silence, none of them brave enough to be the first to touch the food. The bride was huffing. She started to turn, looking as if she were about to leave them alone, but then, out of the corner of her eye, she noticed a new target, so she spun back toward them. "Will you try that table, sweetie?" Jua shook his head manically. Kampol and Oan kept their eyes down. "Help me out, please, sweetie. You can sit down and eat right after." The bride came over to Kampol and made him stand up by grabbing his arm. "But go get the whiskey first. Hurry!"

Kampol grudgingly walked over. Once at the table, he reached for the bottle, nabbing it without meeting anyone's eye. Then he quickly turned around and retreated. But he wasn't quite quick enough. "Hey! A thief!" he heard someone say, and then a hand seized him.

"It wasn't me!" Kampol screamed, terrified. "The bride sent me."

The bottle in his hand was confiscated. After that, he was released from his duties. It became a matter between the adults. The newlyweds were standing side by side. The bride's mother came over to back them up, and Old Jai was also there to support the young couple. The groom's guests had the bride's guests as their witnesses, attesting to the fact that they, too, nearly had the whiskey from their table taken by the bride. The bride claimed that she was only collecting bottles from the tables that were all women, when she saw that no one was drinking from them. The guests countered that what she did showed a complete lack of respect.

"That's right. You invited us for food and drink and yet you want to take it back. If you didn't want us here, then why did you invite us?"

"Of course we're giving you food and drink. But why should people who aren't drinking hold onto a bottle of whiskey?"

"Still, you should have waited until we left the table before you rounded them up."

"Some people were eyeing them to take them home for their husbands, that's why…"

The children waited to see how the drama was going to unfold, braced for something gruesome to go down right before their eyes.

Old Gan, with his shirt tied around his head, flung his flip-flops to the ground, took a couple of guarded steps over to the problematic bottle of whiskey, snatched it, unscrewed the cap, and raised it over his head.

"Everybody, listen here," he said, projecting his voice, which was shaky but full of courage, capturing the attention of every guest at the reception. "Today is an auspicious day. Let's keep calm. Don't let your tempers get the better of you. We came together today to help celebrate this couple, so please let's keep the spirit going. Let's not argue in the middle of this happy occasion. As for this troublemaker of a bottle, I'll deal with it myself!"

With his stance wide and firm, Old Gan tipped the bottle of whiskey over his mouth. All around him, people were slack-jawed. And he held the bottle steady that way, the whiskey pouring into his mouth. Old Jai, snapping to attention, grabbed another bottle of whiskey and took his place beside his buddy.

"Like my friend said, keep the spirit of solidarity going, my brothers and sisters, for the sake of this auspicious occasion." Then he, too, tilted his bottle.

Later that evening, Old Jai and some of his family members arrived back in the neighborhood from the wedding. The young men among them carried the father of the groom and his best friend from the pickup truck into Old Jai's house. There they lay, side by side, completely zonked out. In his hands, Old Gan was still clutching his new pair of flip-flops. Old Jai had lost his, no one remembered where.

Kampol, Oan, and Jua, about to drop, dragged themselves home. People called out to them from every direction as they walked, wanting to know if the wedding had been fun.

Mama's Back

On a sunny Saturday morning, Kampol and Oan were shaking out their school uniforms and hanging them up in front of the house. The clothesline was too high for them to reach, so they were using a chair. The two of them took turns climbing up and then jumping down, hanging the clothes one by one.

"Hey, isn't that your mama?" Oan said from atop the chair, peering up the road.

"Where?" Kampol asked, yanking him down from the chair and taking his place. Elevated, Kampol stared with such intensity that his eyes practically popped out. It was indeed his mother, still a ways away, on the road. She turned and disappeared into Mrs. Tongjan's house. Kampol's heart was racing but he didn't say a word. He kept his eyes fixed on where she'd been, even though she was out of sight.

"Hey, why don't you go see her?" Oan asked, but Kampol shook his head and began hanging the laundry again.

Namfon Changsamran was back. Kampol needed time to adapt to the idea. His mother had come back to see him, just like he'd been hoping and dreaming. But something had changed. Kampol couldn't quite put his finger on what it was. All he was able to think of was that something essential, whatever it was, still existed between him and his father, but between him and his mother it had vanished. And since he couldn't explain it properly, he didn't know how to bring it back.

Because it was missing, Kampol didn't feel like running to her or calling out to her. Even when she came over to hug him, he didn't lift his arms to embrace her back.

Mrs. Tongjan showed Namfon to a vacant unit; the last tenant had just recently moved out. Suddenly, all the household things that had been taken away from him were back. The neighbors all around told Kampol how thrilled they were for him, but he mostly felt thrown off by the new situation, and he would have to adjust to it. As for Namfon, she was constantly weeping, as if racked by guilt all the time, even though she kept up an endless list of tasks to take care of.

Kampol kept close to his mother, eating with her and sleeping by her side. In the middle of her first night back, he was startled awake.

"Fon! Fon! Hurry up and open the door!" a man said, knocking loudly.

Namfon, sitting up on the mattress and crying, answered, "You should leave. I'm not opening the door for you." Her voice was shaking.

"I want to talk to you."

"You should go."

"How can I just leave? I had to go around knocking on random doors until I finally found you. Just open the door, Fon, so we can talk. I just want to have two or three words with you."

"I don't have anything to say. You know how I feel already."

"I know. About that, I know. I admitted it, didn't I? So why can't we work it out?"

"I told you ages ago that I have to look after my son."

"Your son's not the problem. Just open the door first so we can talk."

"I said for you to go. We're over. I want to be with my son."

"I just want to know why you had to run off."

"You already know why. You already know full well."

"No, I don't. I just want to talk about it."

"You admitted that you know."

"What did I admit?... No, that was something else."

"It's the same thing. You know it's the same thing."

"Open the door, Fon. I really, really don't know."

"You know. I know you know."

In the dark, Kampol's eyes were wide and his heart was pounding. He kept still, listening. He listened to every word. An hour later, nothing had changed: they continued talking, on and on, in circles like that. Kampol didn't understand a thing. He couldn't decipher the conversation, so he finally quit paying attention and closed his eyes. But he couldn't fall back asleep because his mother was still sobbing, and her argument with the man continued like an echo in his ears:

"Why did you have to run off? Why?"

"I told you, I want to be with my son."

"Your son isn't the problem. You can be with your son if you want, but why did you run off?"

"Why are you asking when you already know?"

"I really don't. Just open the door, please. It's late. I have an early shift."

"Just go. We're over, and you already know it."

"I don't know that. That's why I'm asking you."

Kampol kept listening for a long time, all the while thinking about how morning was approaching, that the sun was about to rise and it would be light out. He lay waiting, but the dark of the night lingered, with the words and the weeping. Then, very quietly, sleepiness tiptoed in; it appeared unnoticed, even by him. It crawled onto the mattress, held him to its chest, and sang a silent lullaby that drowned out every other sound in the world. Kampol fell asleep waiting for the first light of dawn.

The next day was Sunday, and Kampol woke up very late, with the sun's glare coming through the window. He lay with his eyes open, trying to sort between his dreams and reality. Then he heard a noise from the back of the house and got up to have a look.

Namfon turned her face toward him. He saw how red her nose was, and her eyes were puffy. She smiled and then turned back to the fish she was frying.

Kampol watched her for a long time.

Kampol, His Mama, His Papa, and That Man

That Sunday, Kampol brought his homework over to the grocery store to do it there. He wasn't as cheery as would have been expected.

"How's it going, Boy? Where'd you sleep last night?" Chong's customers all asked with a smile when they came by to do their shopping.

"With my mother," Kampol muttered, not looking up from his school books. The adults, assuming all was well now that Namfon was back, didn't notice the sadness in his voice and eyes.

Once Kampol had finished his homework, he checked in with his friends who were playing under the poinciana tree. Then he felt like having a snack but didn't have the money for it, so he walked over to Dang's.

He brightened up when he saw that Dang was home. "You feeling tight? You need a massage?"

"Lately, it hasn't been so bad," Dang said. "You want to get a snack, don't you? Why don't you ask your mama for some money? She's back, isn't she?"

Kampol nodded, quietly turned around, and walked away. He had thought about asking his mother but was afraid to, so he wandered from house to house, in case somebody might have a chore for him. But all the grown-ups had the same suggestion as Dang, so he strolled back over to the grocery and watched the game his friends were playing.

Then something made his face light up: his father's water truck was roaring into the neighborhood.

Kampol wasted no time telling him everything: "Mama's back, Papa. She brought all our stuff back, but we're not in our old apartment. We're in a new one over there."

Wasu's eyes went wide—from happiness or sheer surprise, it was impossible to say. "Really?"

"Really. Last night, I spent the night with her."

"Did she bring someone with her?"

Kampol shook his head. "She came back alone, but late last night a man showed up, knocking on the door. She told him to go away, that she wasn't going to open the door for him."

"And then?"

"I don't know. I fell asleep."

Wasu paused for a moment to process. "So…when you woke up this morning, was the man there?" When Kampol shook his head, Wasu again didn't show an immediate reaction.

"Papa, come back and live with us," Kampol said. "And bring Jon, too. We can all be together like we used to be."

His father sighed. But seeing Kampol's sorry face and his pleading eyes, he said, "How about this? Go get Mama. Tell her I want to talk to her."

"Okay," Kampol said, and immediately took off sprinting. Within a breath's time, he was back with his report: "Mama said to tell you to come to the house to talk."

Wasu, perched on the footboard of his truck, realized as

he looked up that he'd become the focus of attention, which made it all the more difficult for him to be the one to cave in and make the long walk over to talk to Kampol's mother.

"Boy, tell your mama…um, if she wants my help with anything, I'm here to talk."

Kampol ran back over to the apartment. When he came back, he said, "Mama said there's nothing."

Wasu sighed. He needed a new plan. "Ask her if she wants help paying the rent."

Kampol wiped the sweat from his forehead, ran over, and then walked back. "Mama says there's no need."

Wasu frowned, eyes narrow. He stood up, hands on his hips. "I better get out of here. If I stick around any longer, your mama might get a few bruises."

Kampol's eyes clung to the sky-blue water truck as it zoomed away. When it was finally out of sight, he started to make his way back home. But he turned around before he reached the house and went through the open lot, past the poinciana and the store. Behind Mrs. Tongjan's house, Kampol crawled under his usual shrub and curled up; he stayed there almost until sundown.

That night, Kampol slept beside his mother again, and, as the night before, he was startled awake in the dark.

"Fon, are you asleep? Will you open the door?"

Kampol recognized the voice. His mother sat up, and the same sequence of events replayed all over again. Kampol pulled the blanket over his head and plugged his ears with his fingers, but their voices resounded in the dark room, still sharp. Both the man and Kampol's mother just repeated the same words over and over again.

Monday night, Kampol slept beside his mother for the third night in a row and was startled awake for the third time.

He had begun to get used to the routine, and it no longer frightened him. He lay listening, unperturbed, and fell back asleep before long.

Tuesday night, Kampol slept beside his mother for the fourth night. Again, he woke up in the dark, but tonight was different from the ones that came before. The man's voice didn't come from outside the door, there wasn't the same back and forth. All that was left was the sound of his mother's sobbing, which was louder than it had been on any of the previous nights.

On Wednesday, Kampol came home from school to an empty house.

His mother had gone.

The sun was about to set, and Kampol didn't know where to spend the night. As he stood adrift in the middle of the vacant lot, he heard Chong's voice calling him from the grocery.

"Boy, why don't you sleep here tonight?"

And then: "Or you could come sleep over at my house!" Oan was saying.

"Boy," Jua said, limping over to him. "My grandpa just bought a new mosquito net. It's pink and even has a door for getting in and out."

And that was how, on Wednesday night, Kampol wound up under a new mosquito net with Jua. As they got into bed Oan showed up, asking to have a sleepover with them, too.

The Dignity of a Dog Named Tiger

Every afternoon, on their way home from school, Kampol and Oan passed a wooden house on stilts. It was about head-high from the ground and surrounded by a wooden fence, solid and secure. If you peeked through one of the slits in the fence, you saw a large dark-brown dog with short hair, sitting on the terrace with his head held high. If the boys happened to make too much noise, the dog would immediately make his presence known with a menacing bark. Kampol and Oan liked to peep in at him, and then when he woofed they would dash away.

Once, the two of them were heading home later than usual, and happened to see the owner of the house. She was a short middle-aged woman with fair skin, curly hair, and a lazy eye. As soon as she opened the gate wide enough to let herself through, the dog bounded right up to her, making noises like a babbling child, and jumped up, licking her face, her lips. He ran in circles and jumped on her some more. His short mistress laughed as she hugged him. The homely, middle-aged lady and her large handsome dog were the only inhabitants of the house.

Shortly thereafter, something changed. Kampol and Oan would walk by with trepidation because the gate was left open. The large dog, his ears erect, stared at them from the terrace. The two boys were scared that he would charge them. Every day, the gate stayed open. Grass began to grow on the walkway that ran to the foot of the stairs leading up to the house. And no matter how late they were going home, they never saw the short lady again.

Weeds began to grow wild under the house. The big brown dog, meanwhile, continued keeping watch from the terrace.

Kampol tried to be friends with the dog by tossing him a roll of bread each day. The dog was no glutton, though, and didn't allow anyone to come near him. He only ate when no one was watching. And if you ventured even a couple of steps beyond the perimeter of the fence, he would start growling scarily.

Word of the dog's abandonment began to spread, and lots of people were interested in making him their pet. An older boy, a sixth-grader at Kampol's school, declared that he would be the dog's owner. He lived nearby, not far from the wooden house.

"He's called Sua. Don't go in there. He doesn't like kids," the boy said.

"Yesterday, the lottery seller also said she was going to adopt it," Oan said.

"The man who runs the junk shop, too. He said he wanted him to be a watchdog for his store. He feeds him every day," Kampol told them.

"Nobody knows the dog better than I do," the older boy said. "He doesn't warm up to people easily. You have to be patient. When Auntie Juk first got him, three months went by before Sua even let her pet his head a little. It was six months before she could hug him."

"And where did Auntie Juk go? Why did she leave Sua behind?"

"She didn't want to, but she had to sell the house. Auntie Juk had to move in with her younger sister. She lives in a tall building where they don't allow dogs."

"She shouldn't have left him."

"He loves her like she was his own mother. Sua doesn't believe it yet that he's been abandoned. We'll have to wait until he wraps his mind around it, until he stops waiting. Only then will he open up to other people. If someone wants him they'll have to be patient. I know him well, but Auntie Juk thinks of him only as a dog. If she thought of him as her child, she wouldn't have abandoned him."

Kampol, eyebrows dropping, blinked rapidly as he listened.

The neighbors left an abundance of food out to lure him, but Sua grew increasingly thin. His fur, once clean, became filthy and matted. His stocky elegance slowly diminished. One by one, the people who had tried to forge a bond with him withdrew, and Sua still refused to submit to anyone's friendship, holding out for his mother's return.

The changes continued. A contractor brought in workers to tear down the fence and the house. Sua ran wildly around the property, panicked. He barked, he howled, he grunted, he growled. Only when the sun was low and the workers had left for the day did he quiet down. By then, the fence and the house were no longer standing. Even the overgrown grass had been trampled flat to the ground. On one corner of the property, the workers had built a corrugated iron shed to take breaks from the sun or rain. Boards that had been part of the fence and house were piled near the shed. Sua sniffed around. He decided to use the pile of wood—the last remnants of the house—as the place to sit and continue waiting for his mother. Occasionally, he scaled the whole heap and sat atop with his head held high. Mostly, though, he avoided people's eyes by staying in a pit he'd dug under the pile. Kampol and his friends began to forget about him.

One day, though, on their way home from school, Kampol and Oan came across Sua running down the side of the road. The dog paused periodically to rummage through overflowing garbage cans. Then he went back home, or back to the remains of his home. Construction had begun on the land that was otherwise empty except for the shed. The pile of wood had disappeared. There were only a few rotting wallboards and the depression that had once been Sua's lair remaining.

Kampol took out some bread and stepped closer, little by little. Sua was crouched in what was left of his hole, watching Kampol without moving. Kampol held out the bread as far as his arm would reach. Sua got on his feet, and Oan jumped, shouting to his friend to be careful. Kampol was trembling but kept his courage. Sua approached and, though still vigilant, took the bread from Kampol's hand. Kampol pet his head. Sua backed away. He peered at Kampol for a second, then he turned and went back to his pit with the bread. Kampol and Oan looked at each other and grinned.

When they passed by the older boy's house, the two were so eager to tell him about what had happened that they talked over each other.

"Sua's given in. He ate bread from my hand, and let me pet his head, too. He believes now that he's been abandoned. He's quit waiting. Why don't you go get him and bring him home?"

The older boy laughed at them.

"You idiots, you pet its head with your bare hands?

Haven't you seen how it's got scabies all over it? If you want it you can have it. Be my guest."

Kampol and Oan walked home, still exhilarated by having won Sua over, but confused and sad at the same time.

Quiet, Please!

The grown-ups were constantly warning the kids not to bother Bangkerd the mortician.

Chong was emphatic that they mustn't make a lot of noise outside his apartment, because Bangkerd needed to sleep during the day. Dum told them the mortician kept a ghost inside his home, and Keow, the mortician's next-door neighbor, said she'd heard fits of yelling, which sounded like he was tussling with something or someone to her.

But the prohibition might as well have been encouragement. The children liked to snoop around in front of the mortician's home. They were careful not to make noise in the beginning. Their routine was to crouch low and lean against the wall under his window, then poke their heads one by one carefully over the edge and peek between the glass louvers into the room.

"He's sleeping," Oan whispered after he retreated.

It was Kampol's turn to poke his head up. Huddling back down, he told everyone: "He's got joss sticks burning on his Buddha stand."

Ploy stood up and then very quickly withdrew. "He's not asleep. His eyes are open."

Jua rose then ducked down. "He's up."

"He's up? What's he doing? Is he fighting a ghost?"

Kampol stood for another look and stayed up. "Nobody there," he reported to his friends.

Everybody stood up. All of them tried to shove the others out of the way as they clung to the grating on the mortician's window, fighting for a view between the panes of glass. All they saw was an empty bed and an empty room. They caught a whiff of burning incense. Then, all of a sudden, the door flew open. The children jumped back screaming, and when the mortician emerged wielding a baton, the group exploded in every direction. But the mortician managed to grab only one of the kids by his collar.

Jua shrieked, his mouth stretched wide. You could hear him all the way to Chong's store.

"Quiet!" the mortician barked. "I said, quiet!"

Jua shut up but couldn't stop sniveling. His face was wet with tears.

"How many times have I told you all not to play around here? Why don't you ever listen?"

"I wasn't playing," Jua replied. He glanced over at his friends, who had regrouped a safe distance away and were watching him suffer. "Those kids over there brought me to come and look."

"If you want to look at me so desperately, then look!" Jua did his best to yank his face left and right but the mortician had it clutched tight and forced Jua to look at him straight on. "And don't cry," he growled when he saw Jua's face rumple. "Get your eyeful, and don't you dare blink. If you blink, I'm going to knock you on the head."

Jua didn't last more than a second staring at the mortician. He cracked, struggling and screaming for his life.

The mortician let go. He sighed as he watched Jua limping away. Then he turned and went back inside, smiling to himself. Finally, he was going to get plenty of sleep—it had been three nights in a row he had had to stay up at the temple to ensure that incense burned continuously by the casket.

"He forced me to look him right in the eye. And he wouldn't let me blink. He said if I did, he was going to club my head with the baton," Jua told his friends.

"I suspect Uncle Kerd's been possessed by a ghost," Noi said, his expression darkly serious.

Everybody's heart pounded.

"He doesn't know it. We've got to help him," he said.

And so again—very quietly—the children tiptoed back.

Kerd the mortician was about to cross into sweet slumber when he sensed something flickering at his window. But he was dead tired and determined to keep his eyes shut and ignore it. Beneath his lids, though, his fury and his fatigue were doing battle, and soon enough the former triumphed over the latter.

But not for long: sheer exhaustion came back and brought his rage to its knees. The mortician couldn't fall asleep, but he also didn't have the energy to get up. He could do nothing but lie still, staring at the ceiling.

A short while into their stakeout, the children grew concerned about the inert body lying on the bed with its eyes stuck open. Their whispering started to grow louder and louder: "He's dead."

"Let's try calling out to him," one of them said.

"Uncle! Uncle Kerd!" Noi yelled.

The mortician moved his head slightly, shifting his gaze from the ceiling to the children at the window. He was trying to think of a solution whereby he could sleep in peace, without the children disturbing him, since both warnings and threats had failed. Since he was coming up empty, he simply lay still, looking at the kids all bunched together at his window, sticking their noses against it.

The children, joining forces in a chorus now, called out to him. Because they weren't getting a reply, they felt they needed to try a new tactic. Kampol went and tried the doorknob, reporting back that the door wasn't locked. All of them barged in. They surrounded the mortician's bed, shouting his name and shaking him.

The mortician, utterly hopeless, closed his eyes and turned his head from side to side. He labored to push himself up to a sitting position since trying to sleep was a lost cause. He glared at every one of the children in turn and then groaned, "What the hell are you doing inside my house?"

"He's come back! Uncle Kerd's come back!" The children looked relieved. "You were possessed by a ghost, but it's gone now."

The mortician's head dropped. "Yeah, thanks for your help. Now, please, it's time you all go home. It's about to get dark—you don't want to get possessed, do you?" He looked at the children with his eyes pleading.

By nightfall, the mortician was out cold. Because he lived alone, he had never realized that he was a sleepwalker: he got up at night to fight ghosts in his sleep.

That night, he sleepwalked again, but for the first time he sleep-battled children.

Meant to Be

Everyone teased Kampol, all the time, about a little girl who sold grilled sticky rice. Nadda was six, a second grader at the Samed Temple School, where Jua went to school. She and Kampol were destined to be together, according to all the adults, because she had also been abandoned by her parents. But Nadda had a home and grandparents to look after her. Everybody knew Old Choi, a war veteran who was missing his left leg, and his wife, Jeu, who sold grilled sticky rice and whose left foot was about to be amputated because of diabetes.

"Nad, dear, where's your grandmother? Why are you out selling sticky rice alone?" Chong asked.

"It was too much for Grandma to get around on her foot today, so she sent me out instead."

"Aren't your arms tired? Those bags look pretty heavy. I think there's someone who might want to help you with them," Chong said, pointing at Kampol.

"Hey, Hia Chong," Kampol yapped, a scowl coming over his face, "why are you pointing at me?"

Every day after school, Nadda continued to hawk grilled sticky rice in her grandmother's place. Not only did she look sad, she was growing scrawnier before everyone's eyes. And no matter how the adults tried to lighten the mood by teasing her, she hardly ever smiled anymore.

People got used to the new situation. The person who sold them grilled sticky rice had gone from being sixty-year-old Jeu to six-year-old Nadda. The grandmother did the grilling at home, and the granddaughter made the rounds selling. Kampol hated being teased so he never bought grilled sticky rice anymore.

One afternoon, after Kampol had finished his homework, he went out to look for his friends. Jua wasn't home, and Oan was nowhere to be found. He ended up walking all the way over to the old housing development, where he passed Old Jeu's home. He saw rows of sticky rice on a grill with a thin cloud of smoke rising from them. Kampol looked around but didn't see anyone, so he simply kept walking. Then he froze: someone was calling out. Kampol turned around, went back over to the house, and poked his head inside. In the dim home, he saw Old Jeu—a dark heap on the floor in front of the bathroom.

"Help me, whoever's there. Can you go get Choi?"

Kampol was flustered hearing the old lady's groans of pain. He sprinted up the street and then back down, but he didn't find Old Choi until he ran across and down another street. The old man was playing chess with a friend, who looked to be about his own age.

Choi, frantic, swung his cane far forward and hopped to join it, over and over. Kampol followed close behind him the whole way. A few neighbors came over and helped get the old lady off the ground. A junk truck happened to be nearby; it backed up and parked, and Jeu was carried onto it. She was seated with her back against the bundles of used paper. Old

Choi climbed in and sat next to her, and they went off to the hospital. As their help was no longer needed, the neighbors dispersed. In a daze, Kampol remained standing there, even as his nose picked up the scent of something burning. Finally, he gathered his wits and went to investigate: the sticky rice on the grill had been charred black, but luckily the fire had gone out.

Back at Chong's grocery, a crowd had congregated. Kampol was bewildered by the scene when he arrived—in the back of his mind he feared that something similar to what he had witnessed moments ago might have also happened here. But then he heard Oan's voice.

"Here he is. Here comes Kampol, sir."

One of the grown-ups turned around. It was the principal of the Baan Huaykapi School.

"Oh, so this is Kampol Changsamran? Come here, my boy, come over here."

Everybody made way for Kampol. The principal had good news: Kampol was going to receive a scholarship of four thousand baht to help with his school expenses. The purpose of the principal's visit was to check in on Kampol's living conditions. Having been told about Kampol's situation by a number of the people in the neighborhood, the principal had been overcome with sadness and sympathy. He asked Kampol more about his parents, all the while gently patting the boy on the head and shoulder.

While Kampol was telling the principal about his father, through a small gap in the crowd of bodies gathered around him, he spotted Nadda. She was holding bags loaded down with grilled sticky rice, her eyes melancholy and her head hanging. Her little arms looked bent from the weight of the bags. No one else saw her, because no one else turned.

When Kampol spoke of his mother, everybody hushed to listen. The principal, his expression serious, gave his complete attention. Kampol himself didn't look like he was holding up too well. He wanted people to turn around, notice Nadda, and help her out by buying her grilled sticky rice. Someone should tell her that her grandmother was ill and had been taken to the hospital. And that all of the sticky rice on the grill had burned.

Nadda lingered, looking around aimlessly. Kampol kept peeking at her through the narrow space, growing more and more sorrowful. He wanted to tell her that her grandmother had fallen in front of their bathroom and had been rushed to the hospital, but with everyone standing around him he didn't want to be teased about how he was destined to be with Nadda.

Then she was gone from the little gap.

Kampol was in the middle of talking about Jon, his little brother, but he suddenly broke off, his face crumpling. His large eyes welled up, and tears began to spill out.

The principal pulled Kampol into his arms. "All right, that's enough. You don't have to tell me any more. I understand."

But the more he was comforted, the harder he sobbed.

"From now on, if you need something or have any problem at all, come let me know. Don't be sad, my boy… Now, now, be still. Why don't you tell me what you need most right now—are your clothes, shoes, and school socks still in decent shape?"

In the principal's embrace, Kampol cast his eyes up the road, toward the front of the housing community. He pointed and said in clipped phrases, "I… I want…grilled sticky rice."

I'm Not Just Me

One day Kampol had had enough of his life. During first pe-
riod at school, he got into a scuffle with a girl named Rattana,
and Mr. Sanya summoned them to the front of the classroom.
At the end of it, they were both given detention during lunchtime, during which they were to help the janitor sweep the
cafeteria instead of having recess. The punishment for Rattana
was for one day, but for Kampol it was three days, even though
she'd instigated the fight. To add insult to injury, Mr. Sanya
made Kampol stay after class for a one-on-one chat.

"It's because you're a boy that your punishment is more
severe. Boys can't beat up on girls, do you understand that?
Answer me—do you understand?"

Kampol mumbled a "Yes." He pouted, conceding only
grudgingly. All he could think about was how hard Rattana's
hand had landed on his back, leaving him winded. And when
he'd spun around to retaliate, all he'd been able to do was tap
on her shoulder with his fingertips, because Rattana, that little monkey, was too quick.

"Kampol, look up. I'm being hard on you because I
know you don't have anyone. The other kids, they have parents or relatives around to give them love and to keep them

disciplined. If you want me to get off your back, you have to take care of yourself, you have to learn to keep yourself in line. You have to become an adult sooner than the others."

That afternoon, Ms. Angkana inspected everybody's personal hygiene. Kampol's nails were too long and had black gunk under them, and he had a thick layer of grime behind his ears, so he received raps across his knuckles and flicks on his ears. And even though half of his class had unkempt nails and their skin was just as grimy, Kampol was again singled out to stay after class for a talk.

"The reason I have to lecture you more than the others is because I have to watch over you and keep you disciplined in your parents' place. That is, until you can take care of yourself. I know that at your age, you need someone to look after you, someone to keep reminding you what to do. But if you can do it yourself, and carry through—be it grooming your nails, scrubbing your face, washing your hair—then I won't have to keep pestering you, do you understand, my dear?"

After school, Kampol was sulking, sitting alone off to the side, watching his schoolmates having fun on the playground. There were actually some other children on the benches near him, waiting for their parents; their clothes still clean and neat. But that wasn't how most of the kids were. Most were bouncing up and down, ready to tumble and roll on the ground any minute, their uniforms untucked and filthy, with sweat dripping down their faces, necks, and soaking through the backs of their shirts. Almost all of them were running around barefoot, having stripped off their shoes and socks and left them piled by their backpacks.

Watching them, Kampol felt as though he were observing himself, because he was normally no different from them. Then the parents started to show up in waves. They dragged their monkeys away, one at a time. Some of the dads shook their heads at the running children, clearly exasperated; some of the moms fumed and scolded their kids. But many of the parents appeared unfazed by how rambunctious their children were and how dirty they looked. Kampol watched them, wondering.

When he came back from school, he immediately got a lecture from Chong about not taking care of his things and putting them away properly. Kampol had left his colored pencils in Chong's bedroom and for days on end had forgotten to go retrieve them.

Just after dusk, to close out the day, Kampol got another scolding from Mon, about how his clothes were scattered at various homes and that he ought to have collected them to wash them.

All day, Kampol thought hard about parents, about taking care of himself. Everybody sang the same tune over and over: he didn't have parents, didn't have anyone to look after him; therefore, Mr. Sanya, Ms. Angkana, Chong, and Mon all had to assume the role of his guardian in their absence. Kampol felt like he had not two but four people parenting him, which was more than anybody else had. No matter where he was, at home or at school, there was at least one of them, so he could never hide.

The next day, Kampol was on his best behavior. In math class, he kept quiet and serious and didn't horse around. Mr. Sanya, amazed, couldn't stop smiling. During social studies class, Ms. Angkana cooed over how different he looked now that he'd cleaned himself up.

Mon broke out in a broad grin when she saw how Kampol—without her having said another word—had gone around and gathered up all of his clothes and put them back where they belonged.

But Chong was watching: Kampol played less, seemed less cheerful.

Saturday came, and Kampol's friends were all chasing each other around, kicking up dust in the lot across from Chong's store. Kampol was keeping to himself; he carried his homework to the daybed under the poinciana tree and did it there. Chong watched him from the grocery store. After he completed his schoolwork, Kampol approached his friends but didn't join in their game. Instead, he stood off to the side, his hands clasped behind his back. Chong sighed. He was starting to worry. At noon, he called out to Kampol to come have lunch with him.

"Are you fighting with one of your friends these days?" Chong asked.

"No."

"Why aren't you playing? You were only standing there watching."

"I don't want to get my clothes dirty."

The grocer wrinkled his brow, looking closely at Kampol. "You don't have to be that careful. If your clothes get dirty, we can wash them."

"Okay."

With that, Chong smiled. "Then why don't you go on and play with your friends."

"No thanks, Hia. I don't want to play with those kids," Kampol said, looking Chong straight in the eye. "I'm no longer just me now."

Chong's mouth opened slightly and his eyebrows rose. "Then who are you?"

"I'm both Kampol and Kampol's parent. You don't have to do the dishes, Hia Chong. I'll tell Kampol to do them for you."

Then he stood up and cleared the table.

The Likay Troupe

The likay theater troupe Chalomrak Pakpirom was in town. They were setting up on a small open lot near the entrance to Mrs. Tongjan's community. With their massive, loud speakers, you could hear them from hundreds of meters away. The afternoon they first arrived, the children went by to check out the stage. All they could see was an empty set, but that was enough to make them incredibly excited.

Toward evening, people from the neighborhood all came into Chong's shop all wanting change, and he was cleaned out of every one-baht coin he had in his drawer.

By eight p.m., a packed audience sat in front of the stage. The troupe was putting on "The Thief with a Heart of Gold." The neighborhood children showed up in full force. Mon had reserved herself a spot all the way up at the front. Old Noi and Penporn arrived late, so they were relegated to the back and had to crane their necks to see anything. Kampol and Oan hung out by the side of the stage, watching the ranat-xylophone player work his mallets and snooping on the actors backstage.

The hero of the folk drama was a thief, devastatingly handsome and tall with fair skin, a defined nose, and a thin waist—and the kind of voice that broke hearts. The leading lady, the daughter of a rich man, had large dark eyes that shined, a delicate nose, lips that were sensuous yet sweet like flower petals, milky skin, and an achingly beautiful voice. The fool was short and tubby and looked silly with his missing teeth.

Half an hour into the play, the villain came out and waded through the audience with a large metal bowl, which he stuck in front of one person at a time. You could hear coins clinking against the bottom of the vessel. It was two or three baht, five baht at most; small children dropped in one baht apiece. Everybody stared at the villain when he got close to them. He batted his long, curled eyelashes and contorted his red-painted lips into a smile as he thanked people, his dark-blue glittered shirt shimmering all the while. He made sure not to miss anyone in the audience.

When he took the stage again, it was time for him to battle the hero. He was trying to keep the leading lady away from the male lead, but the handsome thief outmaneuvered him and whisked her away.

Half an hour later, the villainess made her way through the crowd. She held out the same big metal bowl, also taking in two, three, or five baht. She was dressed in a bejeweled purple gown, her breasts pushed up by the bodice and spilling over, and her ample hips swaying with every step she took. Her eyes, lids covered in purple eye shadow and lined in black, appeared extraordinarily large. Her eyes frightened children when she drew close. But she had a sweet smile on her crimson lips the whole time and to each coin she said, "Thank you."

Finished, the villainess went to put the bowl away. When she reappeared on stage, she spoke ill of the heroine, accusing her of conspiring with the thief and then running off with him.

A half an hour later, it was the sweet-faced leading lady's turn to slink around with the metal bowl. She had a coy look in her eyes each time she floated the vessel toward someone. In her dulcet voice, she thanked people unendingly, a winsome smile imprinted on her face. When she approached the men, be they young or old, she stopped and chatted with them in a manner that almost seemed personal. The young men broke out one-hundred baht notes; the old men took out twenties. As her red gown glistened among the women and children, there was a steady stream of coin clinks. Penporn was too mesmerized by her to remember to put any money in.

"How beautiful you are, young lady," Old Noi murmured as she dropped in two baht. Then with a sagging hand she stroked the leading lady's arm with genuine affection.

All of a sudden, the grand Thai house in the background of the stage disappeared. What unfurled over it was an outdoor scene: a lush forest, mountains, a stream, and a little hut. In rhythm with the ranat, the hero-thief took slow, stylized steps onto the stage. The leading lady, who had been meandering through the crowd, hurried off to put the money bowl backstage. In a minute, after the hero distributed his spoils among the poor villagers, it would be time for their scene à deux, flirting and playing hard to get.

Once he was done romancing his lady, the noble thief, stealer of hearts, came out cradling the metal bowl. Smiling as he approached the crowd, he locked eyes—his were sharp and dreamy—with the young ladies, the not-so-young ladies, the single women, and the widows in the audience. The young women parted with twenties; the rest of them threw in hundreds. The children and the elderly put in another baht or two each. An unmarried, middle-aged woman seized the handsome thief by the neck, pulled him toward her, and gave him a loud smooch. He grinned from ear to ear. Before he left to return to the stage, he gave her a final little wave and arched his eyebrow.

In the final scene, the noble thief was killed as payback for his sins. His lady, weeping and wailing, killed herself so she would die alongside him.

Mon discreetly wiped her tears as she prepared to stand up. The curtain slowly lowered to hide the lifeless bodies of the lovers, nestled together. The fool bid the audience goodnight. "We'll be back again tomorrow night," he announced.

The next day, the children were excited, chatting and laughing away under the poinciana tree. Chong, on the other hand, was in a visibly foul mood. The noise from the theater the night before had disturbed him. He hadn't been able to read or hear the TV. He had been able to do nothing but lie in bed, forced to listen until the hero was finally stabbed to death. The rest of the nights the likay troupe would be in the neighborhood—he was simply dreading them.

In the late morning, an unfamiliar face came into his grocery, a plump lady with disheveled hair. She was dressed in a *kawgrachow* top dotted with black mold and a faded sarong. The woman asked for soap, shampoo, and sanitary pads. As she was walking away, it occurred to one of the kids who she was: "Hey! That was the villainess!"

Everyone watched her, trying to be sure. They still couldn't say for certain.

Kampol tried calling out to her: "Villainess lady!" His friends joined in: "Villainess lady! Villainess lady!"

She turned and gave them a smile. The children had their confirmation, yet they still could hardly believe that the woman in front of them was the same one they'd seen on the stage the night before.

At noon, another woman showed up. She was wearing a fitted tank top and a green and red sarong. Her complexion was dull, and she had sunspots all over her forehead and cheeks. Her long hair was pulled back in a sloppy bun, and she had a cigarette hanging from her dark lips. She bought eggs and canned fish.

The children spied on her. Eventually, they recognized her as well: she was none other than the leading lady from the show. They yelled to get her attention, but she ignored them and kept walking.

In the afternoon, a lanky guy sauntered over to purchase cigarettes. Even though the difference in his appearance was night and day, the children didn't hesitate—they called out to him right away.

The noble thief turned and gave them a nice smile and arched his eyebrow twice.

Philosophical Differences

Kampol, Oan, and Jua were walking through the wooded area behind the tenement houses. With the thick reeds rising above their heads, they had to whack sticks left and right to part the grass and make their way through. A way off, on an overgrown knoll, there were three trees that the kids had discovered and often came to visit.

The first was a jujube tree, which bore plenty of fruit, but they were sour and made your mouth dry. The boys gathered a number of the red fruits, which were overripe, shriveled, and lying on the ground all around the base of the tree. Even though they didn't find the jujubes particularly tasty, they liked being able to pick up and eat the fruit as they pleased.

The red-guava tree wasn't very big. The fully grown fruits were only the size of ping-pong balls, but they tasted delicious. The tree grew painfully few of them, though. When the boys arrived at the trees this time, they could only get their hands on two. The rest were either not ripe enough or overripe to the point that birds had gotten there first. The three of them shared their two guavas, each ending up with only a few tiny nibbles.

They were full of hope as they made their way toward the third tree—a wood apple. Over the many occasions when they had diligently checked on it, only once had they been able to sample the fruit. Its bare trunk shot straight up like a pole, so they weren't able to climb it. The wood apples hid among dense leaves, of which there were only two clusters, all the way at the top. The kids could do nothing but hope that the ripened fruits would fall down to them.

This time, luck was on their side. A single wood apple was lying at the foot of the tree, waiting patiently for them. They literally jumped for joy. Oan picked it up and sniffed it, his eyes shining as he smelled its sweet fragrance. Cradling the fruit, they took it over to the banyan tree, not far from the main road. Under its cool, pleasant shade, they smashed the wood apple, and broke it into pieces.

Kampol, Oan, and Jua lay back against the banyan roots, watching the cars go by on the street. All that remained of their wood apple were bits of shell with teeth marks. The three of them promised that they would share ownership of the wood-apple tree. No matter which one of them found one of its fruits, they would divide it in three. Having sworn, they felt a great deal of love for one another.

Oan asked his friends, "What do you want to be when you grow up?"

Kampol and Jua thought for a minute. Kampol said, "I want to be a soldier. You think you two would want to be soldiers with me?"

"Yeah, I do. I want to be one, too," Jua said.

"Jua, you can't be a soldier. They don't take gimpy soldiers. And you, Boy, why would you want to be a soldier anyway? So you can get your leg blown off like Grandpa Choi?"

"If not soldiers, what should we be?"

"I'm going to be a policeman," Oan said. "What do you guys think of being policemen?" he asked.

"They're not going to take someone with a lame leg either."

Oan thought… "How about this—you could work undercover for the police."

"Yeah? Can you be a spy with a bad leg?" Jua asked, smiling, starting to have hope.

"Why not? It's might even be good. Nobody would suspect a gimp."

"And what would I have to do? I'd have to wear a disguise, right?"

"You'd have to spy on drug dealers. Become one of their minions, and when something was up, you'd have to secretly inform the police. Can you handle that?"

"Bah! Easy!"

"What about you, Boy? You want to be a policeman?"

"But policemen get shot and killed, too, you know."

"You just have to learn to draw your gun faster and be a better shot than the bad guys."

"Bad guys can be fast, too."

Oan had to think about that for a moment, but then he smiled. "Don't worry. We'll be wearing bulletproof vests—so what could they do to us?"

"What if they shoot us in the head?"

"Don't be such a coward, Boy. It's not that easy to shoot somebody. Will you be a policeman or not? Say it."

"Fine, all right," Kampol grumbled. But then he remembered something. "Hold up, Oan. My papa told me, when he drives the truck at night, he often gets ambushed by the police. You wouldn't give my papa trouble if you came across him, would you?"

Oan tilted his head, hesitant. "Why don't you tell your papa to drive properly and obey the rules of the road?"

"But my papa said even when he's driving properly and hasn't done anything wrong the police still stop him."

"That can't be. Your papa must have been doing something wrong. When you do something wrong, that's when you get in trouble with the police."

"Oh yeah," something had occurred to Jua, "but what about my mama? She likes to play cards. Are you going to arrest her?"

"Tell your mama to quit playing cards. If she doesn't, I'd have to arrest her."

"Ha! She wouldn't listen even if I told her. She didn't listen to my grandpa when he told her to stop. Can't you make an exception for my mama and let her off the hook?"

"Yeah, and my papa?"

Oan went quiet.

"I'm not going to be a spy for the police anymore," Jua said in a huff.

"And I won't be a policeman either," Kampol declared.

They heard a plop nearby. The three jumped, startled. They didn't plan it, but their heads turned in unison toward the wood-apple tree. They each started sprinting as if there were no tomorrow. Kampol and Oan reached the tree at the same time and grabbed the wood apple at the same time. As they struggled, the fruit slipped out of their hands.

Jua swooped in and snagged it. The other two jumped on him immediately.

The Hairdressers

When they needed a haircut, the people who lived in Mrs. Tongjan's community, both the children and adults, headed over to the shops in the old housing development. The men and the boys went to Mitr, the barber, while the women and girls saw Taew, the stylist. Chong, like everybody, was one of Mitr's regulars, but he chose to go when he was feeling irritable, drained, or listless. There were times when Chong went to the barbershop frequently, getting his hair trimmed over and over again, even though it was still short. Other times, his hair would be swaying at the back of his neck, and he still couldn't be bothered with it.

Mitr and Taew's shops were next door to each other. Mitr was forty-two years old and still single. Taew was thirty-three and also single. Their customers generally rooted for them to combine their shops and get it over with. When they teased him, Mitr would beam, nod his head, and whisper, "I'm working on it." Taew, on the other hand, would just scowl, not playing along. The scenario had dragged on for years, with neither hairdresser giving up their singlehood.

Eventually, Taew started to go over to Mitr's shop for a friendly chat whenever Chong was there for a haircut. Chong wasn't aware that it was anything out of the ordinary. He figured that it was normal for the two hairdressers to drop in on one another. But Mitr knew full well what was going on, and he was always crabby when giving Chong a haircut. Chong grumbled about how Mitr's service was getting shoddier and shoddier. The barber was doing such sloppy work that whenever Chong came home from a haircut, the kids would make fun of the missing bits on the back of his head. Mitr even occasionally nicked Chong on the ear with his razor.

Taew then started to send the children from the neighborhood to take food or other little gifts to Chong after they had haircuts. The grocer, once he realized the situation, grew uneasy. He accepted a gift from her the first time, but after that, he had the children bring them back—though without success. Eventually, he admitted defeat and let the kids keep the gifts.

For three months, Chong didn't get his hair cut at all. But one day he couldn't take it anymore, even though he was still afraid to go to Mitr's. At nine p.m., he closed up the grocery, having decided to drive into town and look for a barbershop. Kampol was staying with him that night, so he got to come along in the pickup to check out the town after dark.

Kampol was wide-eyed with excitement. He couldn't sit still and was constantly looking left and right. Restaurants and bars vied for attention with their bright lights. Chong cruised down one street and up another. Eventually, he came upon a stretch of road where both sides were lined with barbershops and hair salons, ranging from fancy to old school to run-down. They found a parking spot, got out, and strolled around looking for a shop that seemed suitable, eventually settling on a timeworn, wood-front shop run by a middle-aged man, which happened to have no customers when they arrived.

"I'm going to go take a walk," Kampol whispered to Chong.

"Okay, don't wander off too far. And don't cross the street."

Kampol gave his word and was out the door. He headed straight for Cholchai Barber, which drew him like a magnet with its bright, blinking, color-alternating lights: blue, pink, yellow...blue, pink, yellow. At Sakdi Modern, there was a headshot of a man with a snazzy smile, a pompadour, and full sideburns. But when the lights flashed, his hairdo turned into a mass of curls. The lights flashed again, and this time his hair was stick-straight, cascading over his forehead and almost shoulder length in the back. The lights flashed again, and this time the hairstyle cycled back to the pompadour. Kampol kept walking, checking out one shop after the other.

When he reached the end of the small street, he turned around and ambled back, gazing across the street at the opposite side the whole time. He wanted to cross and have a closer look but didn't dare since Chong had forbidden it. The other side of the street was all hair salons for women. Outside of one shop, which had only regular neon lights—nothing interesting—a group of five young ladies, dolled up in full makeup, were chatting. Kampol stopped and stared. He thought he knew one of the women, but he wasn't sure because of the way she was dressed—she looked totally transformed.

Since he wanted to be sure, he yelled as loudly as he could: "Taew!" But then he lost his nerve, thinking he might be yelling at a complete stranger, so he ducked down and peeked at her from behind a navy-blue car.

Taew turned—as did the other four ladies. Still not entirely certain, Kampol kept spying on her, until he heard a stern "ahem" from behind him. He spun around to find a large, pot-bellied man, expensively dressed and sporting a gold watch. "Get the hell away from my car!" the man snapped. Kampol scuttled backward and hid behind another car instead. At the same time, he saw Taew cross the street with a plastic bag in her hand. She approached the man.

"Are you already leaving, *sia*? Why aren't you spending any time with us tonight?"

"What are you selling, sweetheart?"

"Towels."

Kampol listened from his hiding place: Taew was here to sell towels, that was what she was doing. He heard the man ask the price, but he didn't stick around to hear her reply. He dashed off to tell Chong about the encounter.

"Really?" Chong asked, startled. Since his haircut had just wrapped up, he hurried out to see for himself. Without needing to get close, he recognized her; it was unmistakable. Yet he shook his head, incredulous.

"Go over there, Hia Chong. We should help her out by buying one of her towels."

Chong dragged Kampol back to the truck and they headed home. The whole way back, the grocer's brows were knit.

The following week, all of Mitr's clients were trying to console him: Taew had found herself a boyfriend, a sia even, a rich man of Chinese descent. The guy's fancy navy-blue car was parked in front of her shop most of the time now. Once, as Kampol passed he spotted her boyfriend getting out of his car. Taew was waiting for him out in front of her shop with a smile. Kampol rushed over to them, thinking he had bragging rights.

"Do you remember me, sia? You saw me outside the

beauty salon in the market, remember? When you bought a towel from Taew."

Taew's eyes grew wide. Her boyfriend narrowed his, staring down Kampol as if he had a score to settle with him.

Phra Soh

When monks from Samed Temple were out doing their morning rounds for alms, they would stop in front of Mrs. Tongjan's home, without venturing farther in among the tenement houses. It was for a good reason: Mrs. Tongjan was the only one who gave alms with any regularity. For everybody else, it was something they did once in a blue moon, and so if they were feeling like giving they waited in front of their landlady's house. The exception to the usual arrangement was during Buddhist lent, when the number of monks temporarily swelled, owing to a bunch of monks newly being ordained. Near Mrs. Tongjan's housing community, there was only one monk who was a perennial morning fixture. The neighborhood folks never bothered keeping track of his rank. They simply referred to him as Phra Soh.

Phra Soh's strict discipline inspired respect. Every time he accepted food, he said an entire prayer in a clear, loud voice, blessing the almsgiver. He was the only one who adhered to this practice. Everybody knew that Phra Soh couldn't read and write, having never gone to school. Back when he was committing all of the prayers to memory, the first step he had undertaken was to record the chants on cassette tapes.

Then he replayed them over and over, repeating the words to himself. Now, fifteen years into his monkhood, Phra Soh was louder than all of the other monks when he recited the prayers he'd long learned by heart. The people from the neighborhood adored him, admiring his determination. But his illiteracy prevented him from ever becoming abbot of his temple; even when it should have been his time, he'd always stepped aside and allowed a more junior monk to take the spot.

It wasn't only the people of the neighborhood and his fellow monks that revered Phra Soh. Momo, Mrs. Tongjan's ferocious dog, also loved him, acting like the monk was his master. Momo went above and beyond for Phra Soh, treating him like nobody else.

Very early every morning, Momo trotted out of the house with purpose. A short while later, he would lead Phra Soh back to where Mrs. Tongjan was already waiting with her serving bowl full of rice. When Phra Soh stopped, Momo would stop, too, sitting down by his side. Mrs. Tongjan would squat down and raise the bowl of rice over her head—Momo would never take his eyes off her throughout the entire process. After she had risen to give him the food, she would squat down again, waiting for the monk's blessing. As Phra Soh prayed, Momo's ears would stand erect, and he would whimper. Mrs. Tongjan, with her eyes squeezed shut and clearly moved, would raise her joined palms to her forehead once the chanting broke off. When she opened her eyes again, Phra Soh would already be on his way. Momo would keep his head bowed, walking behind the monk and wagging his stubby tail that was no longer than the length of a hand. He would go with Phra Soh about as far as where he'd picked him up—the same routine every day.

Monks out on their rounds for alms either had temple

boys walk behind them wearing alms bags on their shoulders, or they dangled from their own arms those saffron totes in which they transported the curries and other dishes they were given in little plastic bags. The last couple of days, Phra Soh had come with a new temple boy carrying his alms bag for him. The boy was Noi. Noi had vanished from home a week earlier. His mother, Kan, had gone searching for him, crying hysterically. Mrs. Tongjan had seen him each morning, but she hadn't mentioned it to anyone because she didn't know that he'd run away from home. It wasn't until Chong spotted him one morning that Kan learned her son had gone off to live at the temple.

The day after Chong told her, Kan showed up in front of Mrs. Tongjan's house to give alms and ask Phra Soh to take her son under his tutelage. The monk smiled but did not otherwise reply. Noi himself didn't say a word, not even looking at his mother—he acted as though they were strangers. Kan didn't speak to him either. Seeing Noi as Phra Soh's disciple, she felt as if a weight had been lifted off her shoulders. It was something to be happy about. Not only would he have a roof over his head and food in his stomach, he would also receive the guidance and instruction of the monk. Down the line, perhaps Noi might see the light of dharma, get ordained, and receive his education that way; perhaps one day even becoming a monk as respected and inspirational as Phra Soh.

But for some mysterious reason, Momo didn't like the look of Noi, even though they had never had any real interaction when Noi had still lived in the neighborhood. But now that Noi was carrying the alms bag for Phra Soh, Momo, when he saw the boy, greeted him with a low growl. Phra Soh had to call his name sternly to get him to behave. He would quiet down, but the look in his eyes said he still had it out for the new temple boy. Noi was nervous around the dog. When they got close to Mrs. Tongjan's house, he would fall back five meters to let Momo and Phra Soh lead the way, side by side.

After the first month, Noi had noticeably transformed. He now wore a new shirt and pants that looked nice and neat—nothing dirty and shabby like before. His hair, too, was cut short and combed, and he looked different with his face clean and the happy glow about him. His feet, which had been perpetually bare, now had new shoes on them. But Momo's animosity toward him seemed to grow every day. He growled even more fiercely, his hackles raised as if he were ready to sink his teeth into him. Noi kept on guard.

Kan came again to give alms so she could thank Phra Soh. "I'm so grateful, Venerable Sir. You're making a decent person out of him. Oh…I'd love for my son to stay on and be ordained as a novice. Do you think he would be able to do that?"

"Have patience. He's not ready yet. Let's give it some time."

Kan waied Phra Soh, bringing her palms all the way above her head. "Please look after him for me."

Everybody had noticed Noi's transformation, but no one had detected the changes in Phra Soh, even though they were there for anyone to see: a gloom had washed over him; he had the brooding eyes of a person who was burdened by something he couldn't put down and that he saw no way out from under.

Phra Soh dedicated a great deal of effort to try and use his teachings to reform Noi. In the month that had passed, the money he kept in a wooden box had twice gone missing. The other monks had also started complaining about things that were disappearing. Most recently, the lock on the storage room had been picked, and several valuable items had been taken. Phra Soh was more distressed every day. It seemed his teachings weren't taking effect quickly enough; there seemed no way to avoid getting the law involved. Still, Phra Soh hesitated—he felt sorry for Noi, who was only eleven and still just a child. He truly believed that young wood was still pliable.

Only Momo sensed Phra Soh's heavy heart, how the weight of his worries exceeded what he could lift. One morning, as soon as he laid eyes on Noi, he bore his fangs and began taking slow, menacing steps toward him. No amount of admonishment from Phra Soh worked. Noi backed up one step at a time, but Momo didn't relent. Phra Soh saw that the situation was going nowhere good.

"Noi, just put the alms bag down and go home. You can't stay at the temple anymore. The police are coming today to investigate the things that have gone missing."

Noi's face showed that he knew he was in trouble. He took the tote off and laid it down. As soon as the bag was resting safely on the ground, Momo charged him. Noi ran, terrified.

Tail wagging, Momo carried the alms bag to Phra Soh. The monk took the bag from him, put his own arm through the strap, and pet the dog's head affectionately. They walked on, side by side, with a new lightness in their steps.

Boats Are Bigger Than Trucks

On his piece of paper, Kampol had drawn a picture of a large white water truck and was busily coloring in a sky-blue stripe along its side. When he finished, he showed it to his deskmate.

"Somdej, look. This is my papa's water truck. Isn't it nice?"

Somdej craned his neck over. "Really? Your papa drives a truck? Is it that big?"

"It's huge," Kampol said, bragging. Then he leaned over to inspect his friend's drawing. "What's that? A boat?"

"Yeah, it's my papa's fishing boat," Somdej told him. "It's even bigger than a truck. Have you seen one up close? Have you ever been on a boat?"

Kampol shook his head. "I don't want to go on a boat. I prefer trucks. Sometimes on Saturday or Sunday, I ride in the truck with my papa when he's working. You want to come along sometime?"

Somdej shook his head. "Every weekend, I go clamming with my mama."

"What?"

"Clamming," Somdej repeated. "We dig for clams—Venus clams, to be specific—right outside my house. Do you want to go clamming with us?"

Kampol's interest was piqued: "Outside your house—so we're going in the ocean?"

Somdej smiled, bragging now, too: "If you come, I'll teach you how."

The prospect of going clam digging in the ocean—Kampol couldn't stop talking about it for days. When the others heard, they wanted to come along, too, but Kampol told them he was the only one who had been invited. Chong seemed concerned. "Clamming in the ocean? Do you have to get on a boat? What will you do if you fall in? Are there adults going with you? How far are you going out? How are you going to eat?… Maybe you shouldn't go."

On Saturday, though, Kampol was ready to go early in the morning. Chong had packed him a lunch, and he'd found himself a bag to put the clams in. He waited for Somdej at the corner of the main road, where there was a little pavilion.

Somdej's mother was petite and very lean. She was wearing a sarong and a kawgrachow top with a long-sleeved shirt over it. She and Somdej arrived on a noisy old motorbike. Somdej had his arms wrapped around his mother's thin waist; Kampol got on, hanging onto Somdej in the same way. The motorbike zipped in and out of little alleyways, improvising a shortcut to the sea.

In front of Somdej's house, there wasn't what one would call a sandy beach. The muddy ground dipped into a shallow basin, which was littered with rotting seaweed. Beyond that was a bar of mud and black sand—broader than a soccer field. The ocean was a blue swatch far in the distance. It was low tide. To have the tide go so far out during the day was lucky for the clam diggers. When they dug at night the flashlights on their foreheads were the only source of light. There was a smattering of people on the sandbar. Somdej's mother marched ahead, a rake slung over her shoulder. Somdej and Kampol, each with their own rake, ran after her.

"Like this," Somdej told Kampol. He straddled the rake handle, which he gripped with two hands, and then he started backing up. As the thin strips of metal combed the sand, clams were pulled up from the crumbly surface. When his rake caught on something, Somdej would dig it up. It was sometimes a clam, sometimes not.

Kampol tried it. Every time he found a clam, he shrieked. When he finally looked up and around him again, he was surprised to see people everywhere, all with their own tools and none of them paying attention to anybody else. Kampol watched the ones who were doing it differently than the others.

"Why are they doing it like that?" Kampol asked Somdej, pointing. A number of men held a spade or short shovel in their left hand, while in their right they carried a stick with a flat plate on the end, which they glided back and forth over the sand.

"They're looking for gold that tourists have dropped."

Kampol immediately felt his blood pumping. Not only were there clams here, there was gold. With any luck, he might find some himself. Kampol got right back to work; he raked and raked, keeping his head down, knowing that he was racing the other people, who also refused to take their eyes off the ground. The sky was clear; the wind whipped and the sun seared. Kampol was tired, and his arms were sore. He wanted to run toward the sea in the distance. But he fought back the urge because he wanted gold. Around him, there were more and more people all the time. The smooth areas, free of rake marks, became more and more scarce, while the raked, crumbled sand spread rapidly.

Close to noon, the clammers ran out of places to dig.

People had mobbed the beach as if a big festival had been planned, so everyone wound up going home with only a few clams. When they went back to Somdej's to put the rakes away, Kampol heard screaming and swearing coming from inside the house.

"Where the fuck have you been? I've got to take a shit. Hurry, damn it!"

Somdej and his mother ran into the house. Curious, Kampol followed them up the stairs. Somdej's mother was helping a man take his pants off. She pushed him up so he was sitting, slipped her hands under his armpits, and lifted him with all her strength. Somdej quickly stuck a chamber pot under him. That's when the cantankerous eyes of the shitting man landed on Kampol. Kampol jumped and scampered down the stairs. He ran to the beach and sat under the shade of a coconut tree to eat his lunch. A moment later, Somdej joined him with a plate of food.

"Is that your papa?" Kampol asked him. Quiet, Somdej nodded, keeping his gaze on the ground as he ate. "He can't walk?" Somdej shook his head. "So he can't fish then." Somdej shook his head again. Kampol looked at his friend. "What about the boat? Does your papa really have a boat?"

Somdej looked up. "Yes, but we sold it when my papa got sick."

Kampol's brows knit as he thought. "And was your boat really bigger than a truck?"

"Yes, it was!" Somdej shouted. "It really was bigger than a truck. Look over there." He pointed at the horizon, where far, far away, a string of boats with trains of fishing nets were tiny objects.

Kampol squinted in the direction of the tiny boats. There was no way he was going to believe it.

Kampol Goes to Heaven

I want to ride the Ferris wheel. "Let me go on the Big Wheel of Heaven!" Let me go on the Ferris wheel. "I want to ride the Big Wheel of Heaven!" I cry and beg, out loud and voicelessly.

My mother tugs at my arm, shushing me. "Quit whining. Do you want to stay or do we have to go home?"

Papa's carrying my baby brother, Jon, and my mother's holding my hand. At the rice-porridge stall, we veer off the main path and sit down. The Ferris wheel is right nearby. I'm not hungry but I make myself take big bites so I can be finished with my food. "After we're done eating, can we please ride the Big Wheel of Heaven, Papa, okay? Okay, Mama?"

"Not me, I'm afraid of falling off," my father says.

"It's sky high, don't you see? Aren't you scared?" my mother asks.

I gaze up at the car at the very top, and there, all the way up there, are Oan and Jua looking down. I see their white teeth as they smile and wave to me. In the next car are the twins, Gae and Gay, and one down are Ampan, Gib, and Bow riding together in one car. On the other side of Oan and Jua are Penporn, Ploy, and Grandma Noi. The other Noi and Od are together; they're rocking their car side to side, and it's terrifying to watch. I point up, trying to show my parents all the people who are up there. I can't stand being left down here another minute, so I begin to yell. Finally, my father takes me to the ticket booth.

"Are you sure you can go on alone? If you get up there and start crying, I'm going to spank you on top of it all once you get back down," my mother says to me.

I step into the car. The door is locked. My heart races; I feel goose bumps. My car takes off, rising slowly. I giggle, waving to my parents and Jon. My father laughs and waves back. My mother is laughing, too. She points, telling Jon to look. The car goes up and up. I look down, farther and farther. My parents crane their necks to watch me rise and rise. The distance between us grows and grows. Then I look up and take in my bird's-eye view of the temple fairgrounds. The lights, the musicians, the roof of the ordination hall, the movie screen, the likay stage, the votive show theater, the crowd fighting for a turn at the raffle-ticket tree. My car is descending. I look for them. My heart stops. My parents and Jon aren't where they were before. My eyes swim: the ground below me is swarming with people. Oh, there. What a relief. Mama and Jon are at the shooting gallery, and over there, Papa's at the darts booth. My car floats upward again. At the same porridge stall, at the very table where we had been sitting only moments ago, Hia Chong is having himself a bowl. I giggle and wave frantically to him, but he doesn't see me. The wheel screeches to a halt—I'm stuck at the very top. As my car sways, my stomach ties in knots.

The Ferris wheel isn't moving. It must be broken; it probably won't start again. I'm all alone, so high up. I try to sit still, but the car rocks nonetheless, harder and harder in the wind. I'm sure I'm going to die. There's no way I can survive. The

Ferris wheel isn't moving. I can't get down. Papa isn't at the darts booth; Mama isn't at the shooting gallery. I look everywhere, searching: all I see are the dark heads of roaming people. The wind is steadily picking up strength; it whirs in my ears. My car is swinging hard now. I cower with knots in my stomach, breaking into the tears I can no longer hold back. I'm cold and my head hurts, as if I have a fever coming on.

I hear the sound of water, the sound of huge waves crashing. There really is water—a flood of ocean water bursts onto the temple grounds. There's panicked screaming, but it morphs into laughter. Everybody's swimming and having a great time. The water rises higher and higher. I tremble helplessly. Right before my eyes, the water eats Hia Chong, who had been sitting at his table eating rice porridge. The laughter gets quieter. All that remains is the swiftly rising deluge. Eventually, I hear it slosh against the bottom of my car. I close my eyes and wait to drown.

"Kampol! Kampol!" Somdej yelled, shaking him. "Let's go home. My mama will drop you off."

Kampol was stuck in his dream. He heard himself being called but couldn't see where the voice was coming from. He tried to move his body but couldn't—it was stiff because he was so cold. He thought he was about to die.

Somdej's mother waded through the water and lifted Kampol from the inner tube. His body was burning up. As hard as the woman and her son tried to rouse him, Kampol didn't respond. Mother and son put Kampol on the motorbike, swinging over his legs to straddle the seat, and then used a waistcloth to tie him to Somdej's mother's back. Kampol went in and out of consciousness, but he remained mostly steeped in the dream.

Somdej's mother parked her motorbike right in the middle of Mrs. Tongjan's neighborhood. She looked around, not knowing who to bring the boy to. Kampol was only semiconscious, but she shook him until her voice got through. Kampol cracked his eyelids and looked around him. He knew this place like the back of his hand. "My house is over there," he pointed. Somdej's mother carried him to the door and knocked.

Bangkerd the mortician answered. He eyed the middle-aged woman before him, confused as to why she was there, and he still couldn't figure it out even as she placed Kampol in his arms. The woman said nothing. Having done her part, she got on her motorbike and left. When their bodies made contact, the mortician realized the child he was holding was burning up with a fever. He huffed loudly and swore, ill-tempered.

"Goddamn it! People are starting to bring 'em to me before they're even dead."

The mortician half walked, half ran toward the grocery, intending to unload Kampol onto Chong as quickly as possible. On the way, Kampol briefly opened his eyes. As soon as he registered who was carrying him, he knew he was dead. He assumed that the mortician was taking him to Samed Temple in preparation for his funeral. He closed his eyes again. He felt incredibly sad. But so many people had lost their lives in the flood. It was for the best that he had died. In heaven, he would get to see some of the people he had known.

Kampol was taken to the clinic. By the time he opened his eyes again, it was Sunday afternoon. One by one, the familiar faces hovered over his: Hia Chong, Mon, Oan, Jua, Uncle Dum, Aunt Tongbai, Uncle Gaew, Rah, Chai, Od, Noi, Gib, Bow, Ampan, Ploy, Grandma Noi, Penporn, Aunt Keow,

Aunt Puang, Gae and Gay, Uncle Dang, and Grandpa Jai. Kampol was touched to see these people again, but at the same time he was so overcome with sadness that he couldn't hold back his tears, for he hadn't expected to be reunited with so many of them.

But Kampol suddenly smiled. His parents and Jon were nowhere to be seen. That meant the three of them were still alive. Kampol sighed, relieved. Now he could rest in peace.